"I cannot let you die in ignorance...

"We don't even know what to call the place we're sending you to, Barker. There is reason to suspect it exists in more than three spatial dimensions. Nobody knows what it is, why it's located there, what its true purpose might be, or what created it. We know it's been there for, at the very least, a million years. And we know what it does now: it kills people."

"Again and again, in unbelievable ways, Doctor Hawks?"

"Characteristically and persistently, in unbelievable ways. We need to know every one of them. Then we can risk entering it with trained technicians. But first we must have our chart-maker. It's my direct responsibility that the formation will, I hope, kill you again and again."

"Well, that's a fair warning."

"It wasn't a warning, Barker, it was a promise."

ROGUE MOON

"...a fully realized work of art."
—**James Blish**

Also by Algis Budrys

MICHAELMAS
WHO?

Forthcoming from
POPULAR LIBRARY

ROGUE MOON

ALGIS BUDRYS

POPULAR LIBRARY

An Imprint of Warner Books, Inc.

A Warner Communications Company

POPULAR LIBRARY EDITION

Popular Library books are published by
Warner Books, Inc.
666 Fifth Avenue
New York, N.Y. 10103

 A Warner Communications Company

Printed in the United States of America

First Popular Library Printing: September, 1986

10 9 8 7 6 5 4 3 2 1

To
Larry Shaw
Journeyman Editor

Halt, Passenger!
As you are now, so once was I.
As I am now, so shall you be.
Prepare for death, and follow me.

New England gravestone motto

ONE

1

Late on a day in 1959, three men sat in a room.

Edward Hawks, Doctor of Science, cradled his long jaw in his outsize hands and hunched forward with his sharp elbows on the desk. He was a black-haired, pale-skinned, gangling man who rarely got out in the sun. Compared to his staff of tanned young assistants, he always reminded strangers of a scarecrow. Now he was watching a young man who sat in the straight chair facing him.

The young man stared unblinkingly. His trim crewcut was wet with perspiration and plastered by it to his scalp. His features were clean, clear-skinned and healthy, but his chin was wet. "An dark..." he said querulously, "an dark and nowhere starlights...." His voice trailed away suddenly into a mumble, but he still complained.

Hawks looked to his right.

Weston, the recently hired psychologist, was sitting there in an armchair he'd had brought down to Hawks' office. Weston, like Hawks, was in his early forties. But he was chunky where Hawks was gaunt; he was self-possessed, urbane behind his black-rimmed glasses and, now, a little impatient. He frowned slightly back toward Hawks and arched one eyebrow.

"He's insane," Hawks said to him like a wondering child.

Weston crossed his legs. "I told you that, Dr. Hawks; I told you the moment we pulled him out of that apparatus of yours. What had happened to him was too much for him to stand."

"I know you told me," Hawks said mildly. "But I'm responsible for him. I have to make sure." He began to turn back to the young man, then looked again at Weston. "He was young. Healthy. Exceptionally stable and resilient, you told me. He looked it." Hawks added slowly, "He was brilliant."

"I said he was stable," Weston explained earnestly. "I didn't say he was inhumanly stable. I told you he was an exceptional specimen of a human being. You're the one who sent him to a place no human being should go."

Hawks nodded. "You're right, of course. It's my fault."

"Well, now," Weston said quickly, "he was a volunteer. He knew it was dangerous. He knew he could expect to die."

But Hawks was ignoring Weston. He was looking straight out over his desk again.

"Rogan?" he said softly. "Rogan?"

He waited, watching Rogan's lips move almost soundlessly. He sighed at last and asked Weston, "Can you do anything for him?"

"Cure him," Weston said confidently. "Electroshock treatments. They'll make him forget what happened to him in that place. He'll be all right."

"I didn't know electroshock amnesia was permanent."

Weston blinked at Hawks. "He may need repetitive treatment now and then, of course."

"At intervals for the remainder of his life."

"That's not always true."

"But often."

"Well, yes . . ."

"Rogan," Hawks was whispering. "Rogan, I'm sorry."

"An dark . . . an dark. . . . It hurt me and it was so cold . . . so quiet I could hear myself. . . ."

Edward Hawks, D.Sc., walked alone across the main laboratory's concrete floor, his hands at his sides. He chose a path among the generators and consoles without looking up, and came to a halt at the foot of the matter transmitter's receiving stage.

The main laboratory occupied tens of thousands of square feet in the basement of Continental Electronics' Research Division building. A year ago, when Hawks had designed the transmitter, part of the first and second floors above it had been ripped out, and the transmitter now towered up nearly to the ceiling along the far wall. Catwalks interlaced the adjoining airspace, and galleries had been built for access to the instruments lining the walls. Dozens of men on Hawks' staff were still moving about, taking final checks before closing them down for the day. Their shadows on the catwalks, now and then occluding some overhead light, mottled the floor in shifting patterns of darkness.

Hawks stood looking up at the transmitter, his eyes puzzled. Someone abruptly said, "Ed!" and he turned his head in response.

"Hello, Sam." Sam Latourette, his chief assistant, had walked up quietly. He was a heavy-boned man with loose, papery flesh and dark-circled, sunken eyes. Hawks smiled at him wanly. "The transmitter crew just about finished with their post-mortem, are they?"

"You'll find the reports on your desk in the morning. There was nothing wrong with the machinery. Nothing anywhere." Latourette waited for Hawks to show interest. But Hawks only nodded his head. He was leaning one hand against a vertical brace and peering into the receiving stage. Latourette growled, "Ed!"

"Yes, Sam?"

"Stop it. You're doing too much to yourself." He again waited for some reaction, but Hawks only smiled into the machine, and Latourette burst out, "Who do you think you're kidding? How long have I been working with you now? Ten years? Who gave me my first job? Who trained me? You can keep up a front with anybody else, but not with *me*!" Latourette clenched his fist and squeezed his fingers together emptily. "I *know* you! But—damn it, Ed, it's not your fault that thing's out there! What do you expect—that nobody'll ever get hurt? What do you want—a perfect world?"

Hawks smiled again in the same way. "We tear a gateway where no gate has ever been," he said, nodding at the mechanisms, "in a wall we didn't build. That's called scientific investigation. Then we send men through the gate. That's

the human adventure. And something on the other side—
something that never bothered mankind; something that's
never done us any harm before or troubled us with the
knowledge that it was there—kills them. In terrible ways
we can't understand, it kills them. So I keep sending in
more men. What's that called, Sam?"

"Ed, we *are* making progress. This new approach is
going to be the answer."

Hawks looked curiously at Latourette.

Latourette said uncomfortably, "Once we get the bugs
out of it. That's all it needs. It's the thing that'll do the
trick, Ed—I know it."

Hawks did not change his expression or turn his face
away. He stood with his fingertips forced against the machine's gray crackle finish. "You mean—we're no longer
killing them? We're only driving them insane with it?"

"All we have to do, Ed," Latourette pressed him, "all
we have to do is find a better way of cushioning the shock
when the man feels his death. More sedatives. Something
like that."

Hawks said, "They still have to go into that place. How
they do it makes no difference; it won't tolerate them. It
was never made for human beings to have anything to do
with. It was never made for the human mind to measure in
human terms. We have to make a new language for describing it, and a new way of thinking in order to be able
to understand it. Only when we've finally got it apart, whatever it is, and seen, and felt, and touched and tasted all its
pieces, will we ever be able to say what it might be. And
that will only be after we've been through it, so what good
will our new knowledge do these men who have to die,

now? Whatever put it there, no matter why, no human being will ever be able to live in it until after human beings have lived through it. How are you going to describe that in plain English so a sane man can understand it? It's a monstrous thing we're dealing with. In a sense, we have to think like monsters, or stop dealing with it, and let it just sit there on the Moon, no one knows why."

Latourette reached out sharply and touched the sleeve of his smock. "Are you going to shut the program down?"

Hawks looked at him.

Latourette was clutching his arm. "Cobey. Isn't he ordering you to cancel it?"

"Cobey can only make requests," Hawks said gently. "He can't order me."

"He's company president, Ed! He can make your life miserable. He's dying to get Continental Electronics off this hook."

Hawks took Latourette's hand away from his arm and moved it to the transmitter's casing. He put the flats of his own palms into his back pockets, rucking up his white laboratory smock. "The Navy originally financed the transmitter's development only because it was my idea. They wouldn't have vouchered that kind of money for anyone else in the world. Not for a crazy idea like this." He stared into the machine. "Even now, even though that place we found is the way it is, they still won't let Cobey back out on his own initiative. Not as long as they think I can keep going. I don't have to worry about Cobey." He smiled softly and a little incredulously. "Cobey has to worry about me."

"Well, how *about* you? How much longer can you keep this up?"

Hawks stepped back. He looked at Latourette thoughtfully. "Are we worrying about the project now, or are we worrying about me?"

Latourette sighed. "All right, Ed, I'm sorry," he said. "But what're you going to do?"

Hawks looked up and down at the matter transmitter's towering height. In the laboratory space behind them, the technicians were now shutting off the lights in the various subsections of the control array. Darkness fell in horizontal chunks along the galleries of instruments and formed black diagonals like jackstraws being laid upon the catwalks overhead. It advanced in a proliferating body toward the solitary green bulb shining over the "NOT Powered" half of the "Powered/NOT Powered" red-and-green legend painted on the transmitter's lintel.

"We can't do anything about the nature of the place to which they go," Hawks said. "And we've reached the limit of what we can do to improve the way we send them there. It seems to me there's only one thing left to do. We must find a different kind of man to send. A man who won't go insane when he feels himself die." He looked quizzically into the machine's interior.

"There are all sorts of people in the world," he said. "Perhaps we can find a man who doesn't fear Death, but loves her."

Latourette said bitterly, "Some kind of psycho."

"Maybe that's what he is. But I think we need him, nevertheless." All the other laboratory lights were out, now. "What it comes down to is that we need a man who's attracted by what drives other men to madness. And the

more so, the better. A man who's impassioned by Death."
His eyes lost focus, and his gaze extended itself to infinity.
"So now we know what I am. I'm a pimp."

2

Continental Electronics' Director of Personnel was a
broad-faced man named Vincent Connington. He came
briskly into Hawks' office and pumped his hand enthusi-
astically. He was wearing a light blue shantung suit and
russet cowboy boots, and as he sat down in the visitors'
chair, puckering the corners of his eyes in the mid-afternoon
sunshine streaming through the venetian blinds, he looked
around and remarked, "Got the same office layout myself,
upstairs. But it sure looks a lot different with some carpeting
on the floor and some good paintin's on the walls." He
turned back to Hawks, smiling. "I'm glad to get down here
and talk to you, Doctor. I've always had a lot of admiration
for you. Here you are, running a department and still getting
in there and working right with your crew. All I do all day
is sit behind a desk and make sure my clerks handle the
routine without foulin' up."

"They seem to do rather well," Hawks said in a neutral
voice. He was beginning to draw himself up unconsciously
in his chair and to slip a mask of expressionlessness over
his face. His glance touched Connington's boots once and
then stayed away. "At least, your department's been sending
me some excellent technicians."

Connington grinned. "Nobody's got any better." He leaned

forward. "But that's routine stuff." He took Hawks' inter-office memo out of his breast pocket. "*This*, now . . . This request, I'm going to fill personally."

Hawks said carefully, "I certainly hope you can. I expect it may take some time to find a man fitting the outlined specifications. I hope you understand that, unfortunately, we don't have much time. I—"

Connington waved a hand. "Oh, I've got him already. Had him in mind for a long time."

Hawks' eyebrows rose. "Really?"

Connington grinned shrewdly across the plain steel desk. "Hard to believe?" He lounged back in his chair. "Doctor, suppose somebody came to you and asked you to do a particular job for him—design a circuit to do a particular job. Now, suppose you reached into a desk drawer and pulled out a piece of paper and said, 'Here it is.' What about that? And then when he was all through shaking his head and saying how it was hard to believe you'd have it right there, you could explain to him about how electronics was what you did *all* the time. About how when you're not thinking about some specific project, you're still thinking about electronics in general. And how, being interested in electronics, you kept up on it, and you knew pretty much where the whole field was going. And how you thought about some of the problems they were likely to run into, and sometimes answers would just come into your head so easily it couldn't even be called work. And how you filed these things away until it was time for them to be brought out. See? That way, there's no magic. Just a man with a talent, doing his work."

Connington grinned again. "Now I've got a man who

was made to work on this machine project of yours. I know him inside out. And I know a little bit about you. I've got a lot to learn about you, yet, but I don't think any of it's goin' to surprise me. And I've got your man. He's healthy, he's available, and I've had security clearances run on him every six months for the last two years. He's all yours, Doctor. No foolin'.

"You see, Doctor—" Connington folded his hands in his lap and bent them backward, cracking his knuckles, "you're not the only mover in the world."

Hawks frowned slightly. "Mover?" Now his face betrayed nothing.

Connington chuckled softly to himself over some private joke that was burgeoning within him. "There're all kinds of people in this world. But they break down into two main groups, one big and one smaller. There's the people who get moved out of the way or into line, and then there's the people who do the moving. It's safer and a lot more comfortable to go where you're pushed. You don't take any of the responsibility, and if you do what you're told, every once in a while you get thrown a fish.

"Being a mover isn't safe, because you may be heading for a hole, and it isn't comfortable because you do a lot of jostling back and forth, and what's more, it's up to you to get your own fish. But it's a hell of a lot of fun." He looked into Hawks' eyes. "Isn't it?"

Hawks said, "Mr. Connington—" He looked directly back at the man. "I'm not convinced. This individual I requested would have to be a very rare type. Are you sure you can instantly give him to me? Do you mean to say your having him ready, as you say, *isn't* a piece of conspicuous forethought? I think perhaps you may have had some other motive, and that you're seizing on a lucky coincidence."

Connington lolled back, chuckled, and unwrapped a green-leaved cigar from the tooled leather case in his breast pocket. He snipped open the end with a pair of gold nippers attached to the case by a golden chain, and used a gold-cased lighter set with a ruby. He puffed, and let the smoke writhe out between his large, well-spaced teeth. His eyes glinted behind the drift of smoke that hung in the air in front of his face.

"Let's keep polite, Dr. Hawks," he said. "Let's look at it in the light of reason. Continental Electronics pays you to head up Research, and you're the best there is." Connington leaned forward just a little, shifted the cigar just a little in his fingers, and changed the curve of his smile. "Continental Electronics pays me to run Personnel."

Hawks thought for a minute and then said, "Very well. How soon can I see this man?"

Connington lolled back and took a satisfied puff on the cigar. "Right now. He lives right nearby, on the coast up on the cliffs there?"

"I know the general location."

"Good enough. If you've got an hour or so, what say we run on down there now?"

"I have nothing else to do if he turns out not to be the right man."

Connington stretched and stood up. His belt slipped below the bulge of his stomach, and he stopped to hitch up his trousers. "Use your phone," he muttered perfunctorily around the cigar, reaching across Hawks' desk. He called an outside number and spoke to someone briefly—and, for a moment, sourly—saying they were coming out. Then he called the company garage and ordered his car brought around to the building's main entrance. When he hung up the phone, he was chuckling again. "Well, time we get downstairs, the car'll be there."

Hawks nodded and stood up.

Connington grinned at him. "I like it when somebody gives me enough rope. I like people who stay suspicious when I'm offerin' them what they want." He was still laughing over the secret joke. "The more rope I get, the more operating room it gives me. You don't figure that way. You see someone who may give you trouble, and you close up. You get into a shell, and you stay there, because you're afraid it may be trouble you can't handle. Most people do that. That's why, one of these days, I'm goin' to be president of this corporation, and you'll still be head of the Research Division."

Hawks smiled. "How will you like it, then, going to the Board of Directors, telling them my salary has to be higher than yours?"

"Yeah," Connington said reflectively. "Yeah, there'd be that." He cocked an eye at Hawks. "You mean it, too."

He tapped his cigar ash off into the middle of Hawks' desk blotter. "Get hot, sometimes, inside your insulated suit, does it?"

Hawks looked expressionlessly down at the ash and up at Connington's face. He reached into a desk drawer, took out a small manila envelope, and put it in his jacket. He closed the drawer. "I think your car is waiting for us," he said quietly.

* * *

They drove along the coastal highway in Connington's new Cadillac, until the highway veered inland away from the cliffs facing onto the ocean. Then, at a spot where a small general store with two gasoline pumps stood alone, Connington turned the car into a narrow sand road that ran along between palmetto scrub and pine stands toward the water. From there the car swayed down to a narrow gravel strip of road that ran along the foot of the rock cliffs only a few feet above the high-water mark.

The cliffs were sheer and composed of some rough, crumbling stone that had fissured vertically, leaving narrow guts whose bottoms were filled with the same detritus that had been used to form the road. The car murmured forward with one fender overhanging the water side and the other perhaps a foot from the cliffs. They moved along in this manner for a few minutes, Connington humming to himself in a tenor drone and Hawks sitting erect with his hands on his knees.

The road changed into an incline blasted out of the cliff face, with the insecure rock overhanging it in most places, and crossed a narrow, weatherworn timber bridge three car-lengths long across the face of a wider gut than most. The wedge-shaped split in the cliff was about a hundred feet deep. The ocean reached directly into it with no intervening beach, and even now at low tide solid water came pouring into the base of the cleft and broke up into fountaining spray. It wet the car's windshield. The timber bridge angled up from fifty feet above water level, about a third of the way up the face of the cliffs, and its bottom dripped.

The road went on past the bridge, but Connington stopped

the car with the wheels turned toward a galvanized iron mailbox set on a post. It stood beside an even narrower driveway that climbed steeply up into the side of the cleft and went out of sight around a sharp break in its wall.

"That's him," Connington grunted, pointing toward the mailbox with his cigar. "Barker. Al Barker." He peered slyly sideward. "Ever hear the name?"

Hawks frowned and then said, "No."

"Don't read the sports pages? No—I guess not." Connington backed the car a few inches until he could aim the wheels up the driveway, put the transmission selector in Low, and hunched forward over the wheel, cautiously depressing the accelerator. The car began forging slowly up the sharp slope, its inside fender barely clearing the dynamited rock, its left side flecked with fresh spray from the upsurge in the cleft.

"Barker's quite a fellow," Connington muttered with the soggy butt of his cigar clenched between his teeth. "Parachutist in World War Two. Transferred to the OSS in 1944. Specialized in assassination. Used to be an Olympic ski-jumper. Bobsled crewman. National Small Arms Champion, 1950. Holds a skin-diving depth record. Used to mountain climb. Cracked an outboard hydroplane into the shore at Lake Mead, couple of years ago. 'S where I met him, time I was out there on vacation. Right now, he's built a car and entered it in Grand Prix competition. Plans to do his own drivin'."

Hawks' eyebrows drew together and then relaxed.

Connington grinned crookedly without taking his eyes completely off the road. "Begin to sound like I knew what I was doin'?"

* * *

Before Hawks could answer, Connington stopped the car. They were at the break in the cleft wall. A second, shallower notch turned into the cliff here, forming a dogleg that was invisible from the road over the bridge below. The driveway angled around it so acutely that Connington's car could not make the turn. The point of the angle had been blasted out to make the driveway perhaps eighty inches wide at the bend of the dogleg, but there were no guard rails; the road dropped off directly into the cleft, and either leg was a chute pointing to the water a hundred feet below.

"You're gonna have to help me here," Connington said. "Get out and tell me when my wheels look like they're gonna go over."

Hawks looked at him, pursed his lips, and got out of the car. He squeezed out between it and the cliff, and walked to the point of the dogleg. Standing with the tips of his black oxfords projecting a little way over the edge, he looked down. The spray veiled the bottom of the gut. Hanging from two of the projections in the rough walls were a small automobile fender and a ragged strip of fabric from a convertible top. The fabric was bleached and raveled. The paint on the aluminum fender was rotten with corrosion. Hawks looked at them with intent curiosity.

Connington let down his window with a quick whirr. "Barker's," he said loudly over the sound of the surf in the cleft. "He put it in there last month. Almost went with it."

Hawks ran the tip of his tongue over his front teeth, under his lip. He turned back to the road.

"O.K., now," Connington said, "I'm gonna have to saw around this turn. You tell me how much room I've got."

Hawks nodded. Connington swung the car as far around the dogleg as he could, backed, stopped at Hawks' signal and moved forward again. He continued to repeat the maneuver, grinding his front tires from side to side over the road, until the car was pointed up the other leg of the driveway. Then he waited while Hawks got back in.

"We should have parked at the bottom and walked up," Hawks said.

Connington started up the remaining incline and pointed to his feet. "Not in these boots," he grunted. He paused, then said, "Barker takes that turn at fifty miles an hour." He looked sidelong at Hawks.

Hawks looked back at him. "Sometimes."

"Every time but one. He hasn't slowed down since then." Connington chuckled. "You see, Doc? I rub you the wrong way. I know I do. But, even so, you've got to learn to trust me, even if you don't like or understand me. I do my job. I've got your man for you. That's what counts." And his eyes sparkled with the hidden joke, the secret knowledge that he still kept to himself.

3

At the top of the incline, the driveway curved over the face of the cliff and became an asphalt strip running beside a thick, clipped, dark green lawn. Automatic sprinklers kept the grass sparkling with moisture. Cactus and palmetto grew in immaculate beds, shaded by towering cypress. A low, cedar-planked house faced the wide lawn, its nearer wall of glass looking out over the cliff at the long blue ocean. A breeze stirred the cypress.

There was a swimming pool in the middle of the lawn. A thin blonde woman with extremely long legs, who was deeply suntanned and wearing a yellow two-piece suit, was lying face-down on a beach towel, listening to music from a portable radio. An empty glass with an ice cube melting in its bottom sat on the grass beside a thermos jug. The woman raised her head, looked at the car, and drooped forward again.

Connington lowered a hand half raised in greeting. "Claire Pack," he said to Hawks, guiding the car around to the side of the house and stopping on a concrete apron in front of the double doors of a sunken garage.

"She lives here?" Hawks asked.

Connington's face had lost all trace of pleasure. "Yeah. Come on."

They walked up a flight of flagstone steps to the lawn, and across the lawn toward the swimming pool. There was a man swimming under the blue-green water, raising his head to take an occasional quick breath and immediately pushing it under again. Beneath the rippling, sun-dappled surface, he was a vaguely man-shaped, flesh-colored creature thrashing from one end of the pool to the other. An artificial leg, wrapped in transparent plastic sheeting, lay between Claire Pack and the pool, near a chrome-plated ladder going down into the water. The radio played Glenn Miller.

"Claire?" Connington asked tentatively.

She hadn't moved in response to the approaching footsteps. She had been humming to the music, and tapping softly on the towel with the red-lacquered tips of two long fingers. She turned over slowly and looked at Connington upside down.

"Oh," she said flatly. Her eyes shifted to Hawks' face. They were clear green, flecked with yellow-brown, and the pupils were contracted in the sunlight.

"This is Dr. Hawks, Claire," Connington told her patiently. "He's vice president in charge of the Research Division, out at the main plant. I called and told you. What's the good of the act? We'd like to talk to Al."

She waved a hand. "Sit down. He'll be out of the pool in a little while."

Connington lowered himself awkwardly down onto the grass. Hawks, after a moment, dropped precisely into a tailor-fashion seat on the edge of the towel. Claire Pack sat up, drew her knees under her chin, and looked at Hawks. "What kind of a job have you got for Al?"

Connington said shortly, "The kind he likes." As Claire smiled, he looked at Hawks and said, "You know, I forget. Every time. I look forward to coming here, and then when I see her I remember how she is."

Claire Pack paid him no attention. She was looking at Hawks, her mouth quirked up in an expression of intrigued curiosity. "The kind of work Al likes? You don't look like a man involved with violence, Doctor. What's your first name?" She threw a glance over her shoulder at Connington. "Give me a cigarette."

"Edward," Hawks said softly. He was watching Connington fumble in an inside breast pocket, take out a new package of cigarettes, open it, tap one loose, and extend it to her. Without looking at Connington, she said softly, "Light it." A dark, arched eyebrow went up at Hawks. Her wide mouth smiled. "I'll call you Ed." Her eyes remained flat, calm.

Connington, behind her, wiped his lips with the back of his hand, closed them tightly on the filtered tip, and lit the cigarette with his ruby-studded lighter. The tip of the cigarette was bound in red-glazed paper, to conceal lipstick marks. He puffed on it, put it between her two upraised fingers, and returned the remainder of the pack to his inside breast pocket.

"You may," Hawks said to Claire Pack with a faint upward lift of his lips. "I'll call you Claire."

She raised one eyebrow again, puffing on the cigarette. "All right."

Connington looked over Claire's shoulder. His eyes were almost tearfully bitter. But there was something else in them as well. There was something also like amusement in the way he said, "Nothing but movers today, Doctor. And all going in different directions. Fast company. Keep your dukes up."

Hawks said, "I'll do my best."

"I don't think Ed looks like a very soft touch, Connie," Claire said, watching Hawks.

Hawks said nothing. The man in the pool had stopped swimming and was treading water with his hands. Only his head was above the surface, with short sandy hair streaming down from the top of his small, round skull. His cheekbones were prominent. His nose was thin-bladed and he had a clipped moustache. His eyes were unreadable at the distance, with the reflected sunlight rippling over his face.

*   *   *

"That's the way his life's arranged," Connington was now mumbling to Claire Pack spitefully, not seeing Barker watching them. "Nice and scientific. Everything balances. Nothing gets wasted. Nobody steals a march on Dr. Hawks."

Hawks said, "Mr. Connington met me personally for the first time this afternoon."

Claire Pack laughed with a bright metallic ripple. "Do people offer you drinks, Ed?"

"I don't think that'll work either, Claire," Connington growled.

"Shut up," she said. "Well, Ed?" She lightly held up the thermos jug, which seemed to be nearly empty. "Scotch and water?"

"Thank you, yes. Would Mr. Barker feel more comfortable about getting out of the pool, if I were to turn my back while he was fastening his leg?"

Connington said, "She's never this blatant after she's made her first impression. Watch out for her."

She laughed again, throwing her head back. "He'll come out when he's good and ready. He might even like it if I sold tickets to the performance. Don't you worry about Al, Ed." She unscrewed the top of the jug, pulled the cork, and poured a drink into the plastic top. "No spare glasses or ice out here, Ed. It's pretty cold, anyhow. All right?"

"Perfectly, Claire," Hawks said. He took the cup and sipped at it. "Very good." He held the cup in his hands and waited for her to fill her glass.

"How about me?" Connington said. He was watching the hair stir at the nape of Claire Pack's neck, and his eyes were shadowed.

"Go get a glass from the house," she said. Leaning forward, she touched the side of her glass to Hawks' cup. "Here's to a well-balanced life."

Hawks smiled fleetingly and drank. She reached out and put her hand on his ankle. "Do you live near here, Ed?"

Connington said, "She'll tease you and dig at you, and then she'll chew you up and spit you out, Hawks. Give her half a chance, and she will. She's the biggest bitch on two continents. But you've got to figure Barker would have somebody like her around."

Claire turned her head and shoulders and looked squarely at Connington for the first time. "Are you trying to egg me on to something, Connie?" she asked in a mild voice.

Something flickered in Connington's face. But then he said. "Dr. Hawks is here on business, Claire."

Hawks looked up at Connington curiously over the rim of his cup. His black eyes were intent for a moment, then shifted to Claire Pack, brooding.

Claire said to Connington, "Everybody's everywhere on some kind of business. Everybody who's worth a damn. Everybody has something he wants. Something more important than anything else. Isn't that right, Connie? Now, tend to your business, and I'll manage mine." Her look came back to Hawks, catching him off guard. Her eyes held his momentarily. "I'm sure Ed can take care of his own," she said.

Connington flushed, twisted his mouth to say something, turned sharply, and marched away across the grass. In a flash of brief expression, Claire Pack smiled enigmatically to herself.

Hawks sipped his drink. "He's not watching any longer. You can take your hand away from my ankle."

She smiled sleepily. "Connie? I torment him to oblige him. He's forever coming up here, since he met Al and myself. The thing is—he can't come up alone, you understand? Because of the bend in the driveway. He could do it if he gave up driving those big cars, or he could bring a woman along to help him make it. But he never brings a woman, and he won't give up either that car or those boots. He brings a new man almost every time." She smiled. "He asks for it, don't you see? He wants it."

"These men he brings up," Hawks asked. "*Do* you chew them up and spit them out?"

Claire threw her head back and laughed. "There are all kinds of men. The only kind that're worth anyone's time are the ones I can't mangle the first time out."

"But there are other times after the first time? It never stops? And I didn't mean Connington was watching us. I meant Barker. He's pulling himself out of the pool. Did you deliberately place his artificial leg so he'd have to strain to reach it? Simply because you knew another new man was coming and would need to be shown how fierce you were? Or is it to provoke Barker?"

For a moment, the skin around her lips seemed crumpled and spongy. Then she said, "Are you curious to find out how much of it is bluff?" She was in complete control of herself again.

"I don't think any of it is bluff. But I don't know you well enough to be sure," Hawks answered mildly.

"And I don't know you well enough yet, either, Ed."

Hawks said nothing to this for a moment. "Are you a long-time friend of Mr. Barker's?" he asked at last.

Claire Pack nodded. She smiled challengingly.

Hawks nodded, checking off the point. "Connington was right."

Barker had long arms and a flat, hairy stomach, and was wearing knitted navy-blue, European-style swimming trunks without an athletic supporter. He was a spare, wiry man with a tight, clipped voice, saying "How d'you do?" as he strode briskly across the grass. He snatched up the thermos and drank from it, throwing his head back and holding the jug upraised. He gasped with great pleasure, thumped the jug down beside Claire, wiped his mouth, and sat down. "Now, then!" he exclaimed. "What's all this?"

"Al, this is Dr. Hawks," Claire said evenly. "Not an M.D. He's from Continental Electronics. He wants to talk to you. Connie brought him."

"Delighted to meet you," Barker said, heartily extending a hand. There were burn scars on the mottled flesh. One side of his face had the subtle evenness of plastic surgery. "I've heard of your reputation. I'm impressed."

Hawks took the hand and shook it. "I've never met an Englishman who'd call himself Al."

Barker laughed in a brittle voice. His face changed subtly. "Matter of fact, I'm nearly as English as Paddy's pig. Amerind's the nationality."

"Al's grandparents were Mimbreño Apaches," Claire said, with some sort of special intonation. "His grandfather was the most dangerous man alive on the North American continent. His father found a silver lode that assayed as high as any deposit ever known. Does it still hold that record, darling?" She drawled the question. Without waiting for an answer, she said, "And Al has an Ivy League education."

* * *

Barker's face was tightening, the small, prominent cheekbones turning pale. He reached abruptly for the thermos. Claire smiled at Hawks. "Al's fortunate he isn't on the reservation. It's against federal law to sell an Indian liquor."

Hawks waited for a moment. He watched Barker finish the jug. "I'm curious, Mr. Barker," he said then. "Is that your only reason for exploiting a resemblance to something you're not?"

Barker stopped with the jug half lowered. "How would *you* like shaving your head to a Lenape scalp lock, painting your face and body with aniline dyes, and performing a naked war dance on the main street of a New England town?"

"I wouldn't join the fraternity."

"That would never occur to Al," Claire said, leaning back on her elbows. "Because, you see, at the end of the initiation he was a full-fledged fraternity brother. At the price of a lifelong remembrance, he gained a certain status during his last three undergraduate years. And a perpetual flood of begging letters from the fund committee." She ran one palm up the glossy side of Barker's jaw and let the fingers trail down his shoulder and arm. "But where is Delta Omicron today? Where are the snows of yesteryear? Where is the Mimbreño boy?" She laughed and lolled back against Barker's good thigh.

Barker looked down at her in twisted amusement. He ran the fingers of one hand into her hair. "You mustn't let Claire put you off, Doctor," he said. "It's only her little way." He seemed unaware that his fingers were clenched around the sun-bleached strands of hair, and that they were twisting slightly and remorselessly. "Claire likes to test people. Sometimes she does it by throwing herself at them. It doesn't mean anything."

"Yes," Hawks said. "But I came here to see you."

Barker seemed not to have heard. He looked at Hawks with a level deadliness. "It's interesting how Claire and I met. Seven years ago, I was on a mountain in the Alps. I rounded a sheer face—it had taken a *courte échelle* from another man's shoulders, and a piton traverse, to negotiate it—and she was there." Now his hand was toying tenderly. "She was sitting with one leg over a spur, staring down into the valley and dreaming to herself. Like that. I had no warning. It was as if she'd been there since the mountain was made."

Claire laughed softly, lying back against Barker and looking up at Hawks. "Actually," she said, "I'd come round by an easier route with a couple of French officers. I'd wanted to go down the way Al had come up, but they'd said it was too dangerous, and refused." She shrugged. "So I went back down the mountain with Al. I'm really not very complicated, Ed."

"Before she went, I had to knock the Frenchmen about a little bit," Barker said, and now his meaning was clear. "I believe one of them had to be taken off by helicopter. And I've never forgotten how one goes about keeping one's hold on her."

Claire smiled. "I'm a warrior's woman, Ed." Suddenly she moved her body, and Barker let his hand fall. "Or at least we like to think so." Her nails ran down Barker's torso. "It's been seven years, and nobody's taken me away yet." She smiled fondly up at Barker for an instant, and then her

expression became challenging again. "Why don't you tell
Al about this new job, Ed?"

"New job?" Barker smiled in a practiced way. "You mean
Connie actually came up here on business?"

Hawks studied Claire and Barker for a moment. Then
he made up his mind. "All right. I understand you have
clearance, Mr. Barker?"

Barker nodded. "I do." He smiled reminiscently. "I've
worked for the government off and on before this."

"I'd like to speak to you privately, in that case."

Claire stood up lazily, smoothing her swim suit over her
hips. "I'll go stretch out on the diving board for a while.
Of course, if I were an efficient Soviet spy, I'd have mi-
crophones buried all over the lawn."

Hawks shook his head. "No. If you were a really efficient
spy, you'd have one directional microphone—perhaps on
the diving board. You wouldn't need anything better. I'd be
glad to show you how to set one up, sometime, if you're
interested."

Claire laughed. "Nobody ever steals a march on Dr.
Hawks. I'll have to remember that." She walked slowly
away, her hips swaying.

Barker turned to follow her with his eyes until she had
reached the far end of the pool and arranged herself on the
board. Then he turned back to Hawks. "'She walks in beauty,
like the night'—even in blaze of day, Doctor."

"I assume that's to your taste," Hawks said.

Barker nodded. "Oh, yes, Doctor—I meant what I said
earlier. Don't let anything she does or say let you forget.
She's mine. And not because I have money, or good man-

ners, or charm. I do have money, but she's mine by right of conquest."

Hawks sighed. "Mr. Barker, I need you to do something very few men in the world seem to be qualified to do. That is, if there are any at all besides yourself. I have very little time in which to look for others. So would you mind just looking at these photographs?"

Hawks reached into his inside breast pocket and brought out the small manila envelope. He undid the clasp, turned back the flap, and pulled out a thin sheaf of photographs. He looked at them carefully, on edge so that only he could see what they showed, selected one, and passed it to Barker.

Barker looked at it curiously, frowned, and, after a moment, handed it back to Hawks. Hawks put it behind the other pictures. It showed a landscape that at first seemed to be heaped up of black obsidian blocks and clouds of silver. In the background there were other clouds of dust, and looming asymmetric shadows. New complexities continued to catch the eye, until the eye could not follow them all and had to begin again.

"What is it?" Barker asked. "It's beautiful."

"It's a place," Hawks answered. "Or perhaps not. Perhaps it's an artifact—or else a living thing. But it's in a definite location, readily accessible. As for beauty, please bear in mind that this is a still photograph, taken at one five-hundredth of a second, and, furthermore, eight days ago." He began handing more photographs to Barker. "I'd like you to look at these others. These are of men who have been there."

Barker was looking oddly at his face. Hawks went on. "That first one is the first man who went in. At the time, we were taking no more precautions than any hazardous expedition would require. That is, he had the best special equipment we could provide."

Barker looked in fascination at the photograph, now. His fingers jerked, and he almost dropped it. He tightened his grip until the edge of the paper was bent, and when he handed it back the damp imprint of his fingers was on it.

Hawks handed Barker the next. "Those are two men," he said remorselessly. "We thought that perhaps a team might survive." He took the picture back and handed over another. "Those are four." He took it back and paused. "We changed our methods thereafter. We devised a piece of special equipment, and after that we didn't lose a man. Here's the most recent one." He passed Barker the remaining photograph. "That's a man named Rogan." He waited.

Barker looked up from the photograph. His eyes were intent. "Have you a suicide guard over this man?"

Hawks shook his head. He watched Barker. "He'd rather do anything than die again." He gathered up the photographs and put them back into his pocket. "I'm here to offer you the job he had."

Barker nodded. "Of course." He frowned. "I don't know. Or, rather, I don't know enough. *Where* is this place?"

Hawks stopped to think. "I can tell you that much, before you agree to take the assignment. But nothing further. It's on the Moon."

"Moon? So we do have man-carrying rockets, and all this Sputnik panic is a blind?"

Hawks said nothing, and after a moment Barker shrugged and said, "How long do I have to reach a decision?"

"As long as you like. But I'll be asking Connington to put me in touch with any other prospects tomorrow."

"So I have until tomorrow."

Hawks shook his head. "I don't think he'll be able to deliver. He wants it to be you. I don't know why."

Barker smiled. "Connie's always making plans for people."

"You don't take him very seriously."

"Do you? There are the people in this world who act, and the people who scheme. The ones who act get things done, and the ones who scheme try to take credit for it. You must know that as well as I do. A man doesn't arrive at your position without delivering results." He looked knowingly and, for a moment, warmly, at Hawks. "Does he?"

"Connington is also a vice president of Continental Electronics."

Barker spat on the grass. "Personnel recruiting. An expert at bribing engineers away from your competitors. Something any other skulker could do."

Hawks shrugged.

"What is he?" Barker demanded. "A sort of legitimate confidence man? A mumbo-jumbo spouter with a wad of psychological tests in his back pocket? I've been mumbled at by experts, Doctor, and they're all the same. What they can't do themselves, they label abnormal. What they're ashamed of wanting to do, they condemn others for. They cover themselves with one of those fancy social science diplomas, and talk in educated phrases, and pretend they're actually doing something of value. Well, I've got an education too, and I know what the world is like, and I can give Connington cards and spades, Doctor—cards and spades—and still beat him out. Where has he been? What has he seen? What has he done? He's nothing, Hawks—nothing, compared to a real man."

Barker's lips were pulled back from his glistening teeth. The skin of his face was stretched by the taut muscles at the hinges of his jaws. "He thinks he's entitled to make plans for me. He thinks to himself: 'There's another clod I can use wherever I need him, and get rid of when I'm done with him.' But that's not the way it is. Would you care to discuss art with me, Doctor? Western or Oriental. Or music? Pick your slice of civilized culture. I know 'em all. I'm a whole man, Hawks—" Barker got clumsily up to his feet. "A better man than anybody else I know. Now let's go join the lady."

He began walking away across the lawn, and Hawks slowly got to his feet and followed him.

Claire looked up from where she lay flat on the diving board, and leisurely turned her body until she was sitting upright. She extended her arms behind her, bracing her back, and said, "How did it work out?"

"Oh, don't worry," Barker answered her. "You'll be the first to know."

Claire smiled. "Then you haven't made up your mind yet? Isn't the job attractive enough?"

Hawks watched Barker frown in annoyance.

The kitchen door of the house sighed shut on its air spring, and Connington broke into a chuckle behind them. None of them had heard him come across the strip of grass between the house and this end of the pool.

He dangled a used glass from one hand, and held a

partially emptied bottle in the other. His face was flushed, and his eyes were wide with the impact of a great deal of liquor consumed over a short period of time. "Gonna do it, Al?"

Instantly, Barker's mouth flashed into a bare-toothed, fighting grimace. "Of course!" he exclaimed in a startlingly desperate voice. "I couldn't let it pass—not for the world!"

Claire smiled faintly to herself.

Hawks watched all three of them.

Connington chuckled again. "What else could you've said?" he laughed at Barker. His arm swept out in irony. "Here's a man famous for split-second decisions. Always the same ones." The secret was out. The joke was being delivered. "You don't understand, do you?" he said to the three at the edge of the pool. "Don't see things the way I do. Let me explain.

"A technician—like you, Hawks—sees the whole world as cause an' effect. And the world's consistent, explained that way, so why look for any further? Man like you, Barker, sees the world moved by deeds of strong men. And *your* way of lookin' at it works out, too.

"But the world's big. Complicated. Part-answer can look like the whole answer and act like the whole answer for a long time. For instance, Hawks can think of himself as manipulating causes an' producing effects he wants. 'N you, Barker, you can think of Hawks and you as s'perior, Over-man types. Hawks can think of you as specified factor t' be inserted in new environment, so Hawks can solve new 'vironment. You can think of yourself as indomitable figure slugging it out with th' unknown. And so it goes, roun' and roun', an' who's right? Both of you? Maybe. Maybe. But can you stan' to be on the same job together?"

Connington laughed again, his high heels planted in the lawn. "Me, I'm personnel man. I don't look cause and effect. I don't look heroes. Explain the world in a different way. *People*—that's all I know. 'S enough. I feel 'em. I know 'em. Like a chemist knows valences. Like a physicist knows particle charges. Positive, negative. Atomic weight, 'tomic number. Attract, repel. I mix 'em. I compound 'em. I take people, an' I find a job for them, the co-workers for 'em. I take a raw handful of people, and I mutate it, and make isotopes out of it—I make solvents, reagents—an' I can make 'splosives, too, when I want. That's *my* world!

"Sometimes I save people up—save 'em for the right job to make 'em react the right way. Save 'em up for the right people.

"Barker, Hawks—you're gonna be my masterpiece. 'Cause sure as God made little green apples, he made you two to meet.... An' me, *me*, I found you, an' I've done it, I've *rammed* you two together.... an' now it's done, an' nothing'll ever take the critical mass apart, and sooner, later, it's got to 'splode, and who're you gonna run to then, Claire?"

4

Hawks broke the silence. He reached out, pulled the bottle out of Connington's hand, and swung toward the cliff. The bottle flailed away and disappeared over the edge. Then Hawks turned to Barker and said quietly, "There are a few more things I ought to tell you before you definitely accept the job."

Barker's face was strained. He was looking at Connington. His head snapped around in Hawks' direction and he growled, "I said I'd do the damned job!"

Claire reached out and took hold of his hand, pulling him down beside her. She thrust herself forward to kiss the underside of Barker's jaw. "That's the ol' fighter, Hardrock." She began nibbling the skin with its faint stubble of beard, gradually inching her mouth down his throat, leaving a row of regularly spaced marks: wet, round, red parentheses of her lipstick, enclosing the sharper, pinker blotches where her incisors had worried his flesh. "He'll do it, Ed," she murmured sidelong. "Or at least he'll give it as much of a try as any man could."

"Don't the three of you *care*?" Connington blurted, his head jerking back and forth. "Didn't you *hear*?"

"We heard you," Hawks said.

"Well, what *about* it?" Connington challenged them incredulously.

"Tell me something, Connington," Hawks said. "Did you make your little speech so we'd stop now? Or could anything make us stop, now things are in motion the way you hoped?"

"*Not* hoped," Connington said. "Planned."

Hawks nodded. "All right, then," he said in a tired voice. "I thought so. All you wanted to do was make a speech. I wish you'd chosen another time."

Claire chuckled, a silvery ladder of sound. "Isn't it too bad, Connie? You were so sure we'd all fall down. But it's just like it always was. You still don't know where to push."

Connington backed away incredulously, his arms spread

as if to knock their heads together. "Are you three *crazy*? Do you think I made this stuff up out of my *head*? *Listen* to yourselves—even when you tell me it's all malarkey, you have to say it each a certain way. You can't shake loose from yourselves even for a second; you'll go where your feet take you, no matter what—and you're *laughing* at me? You're laughin' at *me*?"

He lurched around suddenly. "Go to hell, all of you!" he cried. "G'wan!" He began to run clumsily across the grass to his car.

Hawks looked after hm. "He's not fit to drive back."

Barker grimaced. "He won't. He'll cry himself to sleep in the car for a few hours. Then he'll come in the house, looking for Claire's comfort." He looked down at Claire with a jerk of his head that broke the chain of nibbles. "Isn't that right? Doesn't he always do that?"

Claire's lips pinched together. "I can't help what he does."

"No?" Barker said. "It's me he's after?"

In a vicious, throaty snarl, Claire said, "Maybe he's had you. He's never had me."

Barker's hand cracked over, and Claire fell back, holding her cheek. Then she grinned. "You've done better than that. You used to do a lot better. But that wasn't bad," she admitted.

"Barker," Hawks said, "I want to tell you what you're going to face."

"Tell me when I get there!" Barker snapped. "I'm not going to back out now."

Claire said, "Maybe that's what he wants you to say, Al. Putting it that way." She smiled up toward Hawks. "Who says Connington's the only schemer?"

"What's the simplest way for me to get back to town?" Hawks said.

"I'll drive you," Barker said coldly. His eyes locked on Hawks. "If you want to try it."

Claire murmured a chuckle and suddenly rubbed her cheek down the length of Barker's thigh. She did this with a spasm of her entire body; an undulant motion that was completely serpentine. She stared up at Hawks through wide, pleasurably moist eyes, her upstretched arms curled around Barker's waist. "Isn't he grand?" she said huskily to Hawks. "Isn't he a man?"

5

Barker trotted stiffly down to the garage apron and flung up the overhead doors with a crash, as Hawks waited at the head of the flagstone steps. Claire said murmurously behind him, "Look at him move—look at him do things. He's like a wonderful machine made out of gut and hickory wood. There aren't any other men like him, Ed—nobody's as much of a man as he is!" Hawks' nostrils widened.

An engine came to waspish life in the garage, and then a short, broad, almost square-framed sports car came out in a glower of sound. "This is my new roadster," Barker shouted up from behind the wheel.

Hawks came around, stepped over the doorless flank of the car, and cramped himself into the passenger side. He settled his lower back into the unpadded metal seat, which was slewed around to leave more room for the driver. The

entire machine stood perhaps thirty inches high at the peak
of its sharply curved dash.

"Hasn't been really wrung out, yet!" Barker shouted into
Hawks' ear. Claire stood watching, her eyes ashine. Connington, slumped over the wheel of his Cadillac, facing
them at an angle, lifted his swollen face and contorted his
lips in a sad grimace.

"Ready?" Barker shouted, running up the engine and
edging his right foot away from the centre of the brake pedal
until only the edge of his cheap shower slipper's cardboard
sole was holding it down. "Not frightened, are you?" He
stared piercingly into Hawks' face. "Are you?"

Hawks reached over and pulled out the ignition key. "I
see," he said quietly.

Barker's hand flashed out and crushed his wrist. "I'm
not Connington and that's no bottle—hand over those keys."

Hawks relaxed his fingers until the keys barely kept from
falling. He put out his other arm and blocked Barker's awkward, left-handed reach for them. "Use the hand that's holding my wrist," he said.

Barker slowly took the keys. Hawks climbed out of the
car.

"How are you going to get to the city?" Claire asked as
he walked past the steps

Hawks said, "I walked long distances when I was a boy.
But not to prove my physical endurance."

Claire licked her lips. "No one manages you worth a
damn, do they?" she said.

Hawks turned and paced steadily toward the sloped driveway.

*   *   *

He had barely set foot on the downslope when Barker shouted something strained and unintelligible behind him, and the car sprang into life again and hurtled by him. Barker stared intently out over the short hood, and threw the car into a broadside. Spuming up dust and gravel, engine roaring, clutch in, rear wheels slack, it skidded down sideward, its nose toward the cliff wall. The instant its left front fender had cleared the angle of the cliff, Barker banged the clutch up. The right side hovered over the edge of the gut for an instant. Then the rear wheels bit and the car shot down the first angle of the drive, out of sight. There was an instant scream of brakes and a great, coughing scuff of tires.

Hawks walked steadily down, through the turbulent, knee-high swale of dust that gradually settled into two smoking furrows leading from the broad swathes that scarred the bend of the dogleg. Barker was staring out to sea, sitting with his hands clenched over the top of the steering wheel, his sweated face plastered with yellow dust. The car was begrimed, still shivering a little from spring tension as it stood beside the mailbox, separated from the ocean by only the width of the access road. As Hawks came up parallel to him, Barker, without moving his head, said distinctly, "That's the fastest I've ever done it."

Hawks turned into the access road and began walking down over the wooden bridge.

"Are you going to walk all the way back into town?" Barker bawled out hoarsely. "You chicken-hearted son of a bitch!"

Hawks turned around. He came back and stood with his hands on the edge of the passenger side, looking down at

Barker. "I'll expect you at the main gate tomorrow at nine in the morning, sharp."

"What makes you think I'll be there? What makes you think I'll take orders from a man who won't do what I would?" Barkers eyes were sparkling with frustration. "What's the matter with you?"

"I'm one kind of man. You're another."

"What's that supposed to mean?" Barker began beating one palm against the steering wheel. What began as a gentle insistent nudge became a mechanical hammering. "I can't *understand* you!"

"You're a suicide," Hawks said. "I'm a murderer." Hawks turned to go. "I'm going to have to kill you over and over again, in various unbelievable ways. I can only hope that you will, indeed, bring as much love to it as you think. Nine sharp in the morning, Barker. Give my name at the gate. I'll have your pass."

He walked away.

Barker muttered, "Yeah." He rose up in his seat and shouted down the road. "He was right, you know it? He was right! We're a *great* pair!"

Sunlight danced into his face from the shattered reflections of the whisky bottle on the edge of the road. His expression changed abruptly and he threw the car into reverse, whining up the driveway as quickly as a chameleon drawing its tongue around and in out of sight beyond the dogleg.

TWO

Hawks came eventually to the general store which marked the junction of the sand road and the highway. He was carrying his suit coat over his arm, and his shirt, which he had opened at the throat, was wet and sticking to his gaunt body.

He stopped and looked at the store, which was a small, graying frame building with a squared-off false front and weathered cases of smeared, empty, soft-drink bottles stacked beside it.

He wiped his face with the edge of his palm, took off his shoes, and stood balancing like an egret while he spilled the accumulated sand out of each of them in turn. Then he walked up to the front of the store.

He looked past the peeling gasoline pumps, up and down the highway, which burned off into the distance, losing each slight dip in its surface under the shimmering pools of mirages. Only private cars were on it, soughing back and forth past him. The mirages clipped off their wheels as they hissed away through them, and melted the skirts of their fenders.

Hawks turned, pulled open the limply screened door with its grimy bread advertisement pressed through the weave, and stepped inside.

The store was crowded with shelves and cabinets filling almost every square foot of floor space, leaving only narrow aisles. He looked around, blinking sharply once or twice as he did so, and finally closed his eyes entirely, opening them after a moment with an impatient grimace. He looked around again, this time unwaveringly. There was no one in the store. A narrow, blank door opened into a back room from which no sound came. Hawks refastened his collar and straightened his necktie.

He frowned and looked around at the doorframe behind him. He found a bell, suspended from the frame where the swung-back main door would have brushed it. It had been noiselessly cleared by the smaller screen door. He reached up and bent the bracket downward. His precise gesture failed to disturb the bell enough to ring it, and he stood looking at it, his expression clouded. He half reached toward the bell, brought his hand back down, and turned around again. A number of cars passed back and forth on the highway, in rapid succession.

He had laid his coat on the lid of a Coca-Cola cooler beside him. He picked it up now and swung back the cooler's lid, looking down at the bottles inside. They were all some local brand, bright orange and glassy red, up to their crowns in dirty water. Saturated paper labels had crawled up the sides of some of them. A chunk of ice, streamlined down to a piece like a giant rat's head, bobbed in one corner, speckled through with the same kind of sediment that formed a scum on the bottles. He closed the lid, again with an automatically controlled gesture, and again there was no sound loud enough to reach the store's back room. He stood looking down at the cooler, each scratch on it filled in by rust, and took a deep breath. He glanced toward the back room door.

There was a soft crunch of gravel outside as a car rolled up to the gasoline pumps. Hawks looked out through the screen door. A girl driving an old business coupe looked back at him through her rolled-down window.

Hawks turned toward the rear room. There was no sound. He took a step toward it, awkwardly, opened his mouth and closed it again.

The car door opened and clicked shut as the girl stepped out. She came up to the screen door and peered in. She was a short, dark-haired girl with pale features and wide lips now a little pinched by indecision as she shaded her eyes with her hand. She looked directly at Hawks, and he half shrugged.

She opened the door, and the bell tinkled. She stepped in, and said to Hawks, "I'd like to buy some gasoline."

There was a sound of sudden movement in the back room—a heavy creak of bedsprings and an approaching shuffle of feet. Hawks gestured vaguely in that direction.

"Oh," the girl said. She looked at Hawks' clothes and smiled apologetically. "Excuse me. I thought you worked here."

Hawks shook his head.

A fat, balding man in an undershirt and khaki pants, with his swollen feet in beach slippers and with strands of wet, dirty-gray hair pressed in swirls against his head, came out of the back room. He rubbed the pillow creases on his face and said in a hoarse voice, "Just catchin' forty winks." He darted his eyes from their hands to the counter, saw nothing there, and muttered, "People could rob me." He cleared his throat and rubbed his neck. "What'll it be?" he said to both of them.

"Well, this gentleman was here first," the girl said.

The man looked at Hawks. "You been waitin'? I didn't hear nobody call." He looked sharply at the fold of Hawks' suit coat over his arm, and swept a glance along the shelves. "How long you been here?"

"I only want to know if a city bus goes by here."

"But you figured you'd just wait until I showed up? Suppose a bus had gone by while you was in here? Would o' felt pretty foolish, wouldn't you?"

Hawks sighed. "*Does* a bus pass by here?"

"Lots o' buses, friend. But don't none of them stop to pick up local passengers. Let you off anywhere, if you're comin' from the city, but won't pick you up 'less it's an official bus stop. Rules. Ain't you got no car?"

"No, I don't. How far is it to the nearest bus stop?"

"'Bout a mile and a half down the road, that way." He waved. "Gas station. Henry's Friendly Service."

Hawks wiped his face again. "Suppose you sell this young lady some gasoline while I think about that." He smiled briefly. "You can search me after you come back inside."

The man flushed. His eyes darted from Hawks to the

doorframe. "You been scr— foolin' around with that bell? Pardon the French, miss."

"Yes, I adjusted it. So no one else could creep up on you."

The man muttered, "I got a sawed-off shotgun back there'd blow you right out the front of the store." He glared at Hawks, then glanced aside toward the girl. "You want some gas, miss?" He grinned. "Fix you up in a jiffy." He shouldered past Hawks to the doorway, and awkwardly held the screen door open for her with his soft, extended white arm. He said to Hawks from the doorway, "You better figure out what you're gonna do, friend—walk, hitchhike, buy somethin'—I ain't got all day." He grinned again toward the girl. "Got to take care of the young lady, here."

The girl smiled uneasily at Hawks and said, "Excuse me," softly, as she moved past him. As she stepped through the doorway, she brushed her left hip and shoulder against the frame to clear the owner's bulk on her other side.

The man pursed his lips with a spitting motion behind her back, ran measuring, deprived eyes over her skirt and blouse, and followed her.

Hawks watched through the window as she got back into the car and then asked for ten gallons of regular. The man banged the hose nozzle loose from its bracket and cranked the dial reset lever with an abrupt jerk of his arm. He stood glowering toward the front of the car, his hands in his pockets, while the automatic nozzle pumped gasoline into the tank. As the automatic surge valve tripped shut, while the pump's counter was passing nine and a half, the man immediately yanked the dribbling nozzle out and slammed it back on its bracket. He crumpled the five-dollar bill the girl held out through her window. "C'mon back in the store for your change," he growled, and strode away.

Hawks waited until the man was bent over the counter, fumbling in a cash drawer under its top. Then he said, "I'll take the lady's change back to her."

The man turned and stared at him, money clutched in his fist. Hawks looked toward the girl, who had the screen door half open, her face somewhat strained. "That'll be all right, won't it?" he said to her.

She nodded. "Yes," she said nervously.

The man slapped the change into Hawks' palm. Hawks looked down at it.

"Ain't that right for ten gallons, mister?" the man said belligerently. "You want to look and see what it says on the God-damned pump?"

"It's not right for four-tenths less than ten gallons. I did look." Hawks continued to face the man, who turned suddenly and scrabbled in the cash drawer again. He gave Hawks the rest of the change.

"Come in here and push a man around in his own store," the man said under his breath. "Go on—get out of here, you don't want to buy somethin'." He turned away toward the back of the store.

Hawks stepped outside and gave the girl her change. As the screen shut behind him, the bell tinkled. He shook his head. "I made him act that way. I upset him. I'm sorry he was so unpleasant to you."

The girl had brought her purse with her and was putting her money back into it. "You're not responsible for what he is." Without raising her face, she said with some effort, "Do—do you need a ride into the city?"

"To the bus stop, yes, thank you." He smiled gently as she looked up. "I forgot I wasn't a boy any more. I set out on a longer walk than I thought."

"You don't have to explain yourself to me," the girl said. "Why should you think you need a passport to ride with someone?"

Hawks shrugged. "People seem to want it." He shook his head again, a little bemused. "Why don't you?"

The girl frowned and shifted her feet. "I have to go all the way into the city," she said. "There's no point just dropping you at the bus stop."

Hawks plucked uneasily at the coat over his arm. Then he put it on and buttoned it. "All right." A trace of vertical shadow appeared in the coarse skin between his eyebrows and remained there. He smoothed the coat against his ribs. "Thank you."

"Let's go, then," the girl said. They got into the car and pulled out into the traffic stream on the highway.

They sat stiffly in the car as it rolled down the road, its tires thumping regularly over the oozing expansion joints in the concrete.

"I don't look like a pickup," the girl said.

Hawks looked at her, still frowning faintly. "You're very attractive."

"But I'm not easy! I'm offering you a ride. Because you need it, I suppose." Her short hands clicked their scarlet nails against the steering wheel's worn, pitted plastic.

"I know that," he said quietly. "And I don't think you're doing it out of gratitude. That fellow wasn't anybody you couldn't have handled by yourself. I only spared you some effort. I'm not your gallant rescuer, and I haven't won your hand in mortal combat."

"Well, then," she said.

"We're trapping ourselves again," he said. "Neither of us knows quite what to do. We're talking in circles. If that fellow hadn't come out, we'd still be in that store, dancing a ritual dance around each other."

She nodded vehemently. "Oh, I'm sorry—I thought you worked here!" she mimicked herself.

"No—uh—I don't," he supplied.

"Well—uh—is anybody here?"

"I don't know. Do you suppose we should call out, or something . . . ?"

"What should we say?"

"'Hey, You!'?"

"Perhaps we should tap a coin on the counter?"

"I—uh—I only have a five-dollar bill."

"Well, then . . ." he trailed away in a tense imitation of an embarrassed mumble.

The girl thumped her left foot impatiently against the floorboards. "Yes, that's *exactly* how it would have been! And now we're doing it here, instead of there! Can't *you* do something about it?"

Hawks took a deep breath. "My name is Edward Hawks. I'm forty-two years old, unmarried, and I'm a college graduate. I work for Continental Electronics."

The girl said, "I'm Elizabeth Cummings. I'm just getting started as a fashion designer. Single. I'm twenty-five." She glanced aside at him. "Why were you walking?"

"I often walked when I was a boy," he said. "I had many things to think about. I couldn't understand the world, and

I kept trying to discover the secret of living successfully in it. If I sat in a chair at home and thought, it worried my parents. There were times when they thought it was laziness, and times when they thought there was something wrong with me. I didn't know what it was. If I went somewhere else, there were other people who had to be accounted to. So I walked to be alone with myself. I walked miles. And I couldn't discover the secret of the world, or what was wrong with me. But I felt I was coming closer and closer. Then, when enough time had passed, I gradually learned how I could behave properly in the world as I saw it." He smiled. "That's why I was walking this afternoon."

"And where are you going now?"

"Back to work. I have to do some preliminary setting-up on a project we're starting tomorrow." He looked briefly out through the window, and then brought his glance back to Elizabeth. "Where are you going?"

"I have a studio downtown. I have to work late tonight, too."

"Will you give me your address and phone number, so I can call you tomorrow?"

"Yes," she said. "Tomorrow night?"

"If I may."

She said, "Don't ask me questions if you know the answers." She looked at him. "Don't tell me unimportant things just to pass the time."

"Then I'll have many more things to tell you."

She stopped the car in front of Continental Electronics' main gate, to let him out. "You're the Edward Hawks," she said.

"And you're the Elizabeth Cummings."

She gestured toward the sprawled white buildings. "You know what I mean."

He looked at her gravely. "I'm the Edward Hawks who's important to another human being. You're the Elizabeth Cummings."

She reached out and touched his sleeve as he opened the car door. "That's too hot to wear on a day like this."

He stopped beside the car, opened the jacket, took it off, and again folded it over his arm. Then he smiled, raised his hand in a tentative gesture, turned, and walked through the gate that a guard was holding open for him.

THREE

1

In the morning, at a quarter to nine, the phone rang in the laboratory. Sam Latourette took it from the technician who'd picked it up. He said, "Well, if he's like that, don't take any crap from him, Tom. Tell him to wait. I'll notify Ed Hawks." He hung up and padded in his old shoes across the floor, to where Hawks was with the crew of Navy dressers laying out the equipment Barker would wear.

The suit lay open on its long, adjustable table like a sectioned lobster, trailing disconnected air hoses from its sides, its crenelated joints bulging arthritically because of the embedded electric motors and hydraulic pistons that would move them. Hawks had run leads from a test power supply into the joints; the suit flexed and twitched, scraping its legs ponderously on the table's plastic facing, writhing the tool and pincer clusters at the ends of its arms. One of the Navy men wheeled up a compressed air cylinder and snapped the air hoses to it. At Hawks' nod, the helmet, crested with reinforcing ridges, its faceplate barred by a crosshatch of steel rods, hissed shrilly through its intakes while the table surface groaned.

"Leave it, Ed," Sam Latourette said. "These men can handle that."

Hawks looked apologetically at the Navy men, who had all turned their eyes on Latourette. "I know that, Sam."

"Are *you* going to wear it? Leave it alone!" Latourette burst out. "Nothing ever goes wrong with any of the equipment!"

Hawks said patiently, "I want to do it. The boys, here"—he gestured toward the dressers—"the boys don't mind my playing with their Erector set."

"Well, this fellow Barker's down at the gate. Give me his pass and stuff, and I'll go down and get him. He sounds like a real prize."

"No, I'll do that, Sam." Hawks stepped back from the table and nodded toward the dressers. "It's in fine shape. Thank you." He left the laboratory and went up the stairs to the ground floor, preoccupied.

Outside, he walked along the fog-wet, black asphalt driveway toward the gate, which was at first barely visible through the acrid mist. He looked at his wrist watch, and smiled faintly.

Barker had left his car in the outer parking lot and was standing on the other side of the small pedestrian gate, staring coldly through it at the guard, who ignored him stiffly. Barker's cheekbones were flushed red, and his poplin windbreaker was curled over his left forearm as though he expected to begin a knife fight.

"Morning, Dr. Hawks," the guard said as Hawks came up. "This man's been tryin' to talk me into lettin' him in without a pass. And he's been tryin' to pump me about what you're doin'."

Hawks nodded and looked thoughtfully at Barker. "I'm not surprised." He reached into his suit pocket, under his smock, and handed over the company pass and security O.K. slip from the FBI. The guard took them into his cubicle to record the numbers on his log sheet.

Barker looked defiantly at Hawks. "What's in this place? Another atom bomb project?"

"There's no need to fish for information," Hawks said quietly. "And no purpose in doing it with a man who lacks it. Stop wasting your energy. I'd be happier if I hadn't guessed exactly how you'd act here." Hawks said, "Thank you, Tom," as the guard came out and unlocked the gate. He turned back to Barker. "You'll always be told everything you need to know."

Barker said, "Sometimes it's better for me if I'm allowed to judge what I need, or don't. But—" He bowed deeply from the hips. "At your service." He straightened and glanced up at the length of heavy-gauge pipe forming the lintel of the gate in the Cyclone fencing. He twisted his pinched lips into a smile. "Well, *morituri te salutamus*, Doctor," he said as he stepped through. "We signify your status at the point of our death."

Hawks' face twitched. "I've also read a book," he said softly, and turned away. "Put on your badge and come with me."

Barker took it from the guard, who was holding it out patiently, and clipped it to his Basque shirt pocket. "And thank you, Tom," he said over his shoulder, falling into step with Hawks.

"Claire didn't want me to come," he said, cocking his head up to glance significantly at Hawks. "She's afraid."

"Of what I might do to you, or of what might happen to her because of it?" Hawks answered, keeping his eyes on the buildings.

"I don't know, Doctor." There was wariness in Barker's tension. "But," he said slowly, his voice hard and sharp, "I'm the only other man that ever frightens her."

Hawks said nothing. He continued to walk back toward the laboratory, and after a while Barker smiled once again, thinly and crookedly, and also walked with his eyes only on where his feet were taking him.

The stairway down into the laboratory from the main floor, where the passenger elevators stopped, was clad with plates of non-skid sheet steel. The green paint on the plates was fresh at the edges, worn off the tops of the die-stamped diamonds closer in. Nearer the center, the diamonds had been worn down to the underlying angled parallel ridges. In the center itself, a freehand pattern of electric welds had been imposed over the thinned, flat metal. Hawks' and Barker's footsteps slurred and rang in the battleship-gray stairwell.

"Shuffle your victims up and down in long, shackled lines, do you?" Barker said.

"I'm glad to see you've found a new line of talk," Hawks answered.

"Many's the agonized scream that's echoed up this shaft,

I'll wager. What's beyond those doors? The torture chamber?"

"The laboratory." He held open the swinging door. "Come in."

"Pleasure." Barker straightened his shoulders into perfect symmetry, threw the folded windbreaker half across his back, and stepped past Hawks. He walked out a few feet into the main aisle between the cabinets holding the voltage regulator series and put his hands in his pockets, stopping to look around. Hawks stopped with him.

All the work lights were on. Barker turned his body slowly from the hips, studying the galleries of signal-modulating equipment, watching the staff assistants running off component checks.

"Busy," he said, looking at the white-coated men, who were consulting check-off sheets on their clipboards, setting switches, cutting in signal generators from the service racks above each gallery, switching off, resetting, retesting. His glance fell on the nearest of a linked array of differential amplifier racks on the laboratory floor. "Lots of wiring. I like that. Marvels of science. That sort of thing."

"It's part of a man," Hawks said.

"Oh?" Barker lifted one eyebrow. His eyes were dancing mockingly. "Plugs and wires and little ceramic widgets," he challenged.

"I told you," Hawks said calmly. "You don't have to try to get a rise out of us. We'll tell you. That's part of a man. The amplifier next to it is set up to be another part.

"That entire bank of amplifiers is set up to contain an exact electronic description of a man: his physical structure, down to the last moving particle of the last atom in the last molecule in the last cell at the end of his little toe's nail. It knows, thereby, his nervous reaction time and volume, the range and nature of his reflexes, the electrical capacity of each cell in his brain. It knows everything it needs to know so it can tell another machine how to build that man.

"It happens to be a man named Sam Latourette, but it could be anyone. It's our standard man. When the matter transmitter's scanner converts you into a series of similar electron flows, the information goes on a tape to be filed. It also goes in here, so we can read out the differences between you and the standard. That gives us a cross-check when we need accurate signal modulation. That's what we're going to do today. Take our initial scan, so we can have a control tape and a differential reading to use when we transmit tomorrow."

"Transmit what?"

"You."

"Where?"

"I told you that, too. The Moon."

"Just like that? No rockets, no countdowns? Just a bunch of tubes sputtering and *squish*! I'm on the Moon, like a three-D radiophoto." Barker smiled. "Ain't science great?"

Hawks looked at him woodenly. "We're not conducting any manhood contests here, Barker. We're working at a job. It's not necessary to keep your guard up all the time."

"Would you know a contest if you saw one, Doctor?"

Sam Latourette, who had come up behind them, growled, "Shut up, Barker!"

Barker turned casually. "Jesus, fellow, *I* didn't eat your baby."

"It's all right, Sam," Hawks said patiently. "Al Barker, this is Sam Latourette. Doctor Samuel Latourette."

Barker glanced at the amplifiers and back. "We've met," he said to Latourette, extending his hand.

"You're not very funny, Barker."

Barker lowered his hand. "I'm not a comedian by trade. What're you—the house mother?"

"I've been looking over the file Personnel sent down on you," Latourette said with heavy persistence. "I wanted to see what your chances were of being any use to us here. And I just want you to remember one thing." Latourette had lowered his head until his neck was almost buried between his massive shoulders, and his face was broadened by parallel rows of yellowish flesh that sprang into thick furrows down the sides of his jaw. "When you talk to Dr. Hawks, you're talking to the only man in the world who could have built this." His pawing gesture took in the galleries, the catwalks, the amplifier bank, the transmitter hulking at the far wall. "You're talking to a man who's as far removed from muddleheadedness—from what you and I think of as normal human error—as you are from a chimp. You're not fit to judge his work or make smart cracks about it. Your little personality twists aren't fit for his concern. You've been hired to do a job here, just like the rest of us. If you can't do it without making more trouble for him than you're worth, get out—don't add to his burden. He's got enough on his mind already." Latourette flashed a deep-eyed look at Hawks. "More than enough." His shoulders arched forward. His forearms dangled loosely and warily. "Got it straight, now?"

Barker's expression was attentive and dispassionate as

he looked at Latourette. His weight had shifted almost entirely away from his artificial leg, but there was no other sign of tension in him. He was deathly calm.

"Sam," Hawks said, "I want you to supervise the tests on the lab receiver. It needs doing now. Then I need a check on the telemeter data from the relay tower and the Moon receiver. Let me know as soon as you've done that."

Barker watched Latourette turn and stride soundlessly away down along the amplifier bank toward the receiving stage. There a group of technicians was fluoroscoping a series of test objects being transmitted to it by another team.

"Come with me, please," Hawks said to Barker and walked slowly toward the table where the suit lay.

"So they talk about you like that around here," Barker said, still turning his head from side to side as they walked. "No wonder you get impatient when you're outside dealing with the big world."

"Barker, it's important that you concern yourself only with what you're here to do. It's removed from all human experience, and if you're to go through it successfully, there are a number of things you must absorb. Let's try to keep personalities out of this."

"How about your boy, over there? Latourette?"

"Sam's a very good man," Hawks said.

"And that's his excuse."

"It's his reason for being here. Ordinarily, he'd be in a sanatorium under sedation for his pain. He has an inoperable cancer. He'll be dead next year."

They had passed the low wall of linked gray steel cabinets. Barker's head jerked back around. "Oh," he said.

"That's why he's the standard man in there. Nothing eating at the flesh. Eternal life."

"No usual man wants to die," Hawks, said, touching Barker's shoulder and moving him gently toward the suit. The men of the Navy crew were darting covert glances at Barker only after looking around to see if any of their teammates were watching them at that particular instant. "Otherwise, the world would be swept by suicides."

2

Hawks did not introduce Barker to the crew. He pointed to the suit as he reached the edge of the table. "Now, this is the best we can do for you in the way of protection. You get into it here, on the table, and you'll be wheeled into the transmitter. You'll be beamed up to the Moon receiver in it—once there, you'll find it comfortable and easily maneuverable. You have power assists, activated by the various pressures your body puts on them. The suit will comply to all your movements. I'm told it feels like swimming. You have a selection of all the tools we know you'll need, and a number of others we think might be called for. That's something you'll have to tell us afterward, if you can. It's important that you thoroughly familiarize yourself with the operations of the suit—most of them are automatic, but it's much better to be sure. Now I'd like you to get into it, so the ensign and his men, here, can check to see that you won't have any difficulties."

The naval officer in charge of the specialist crew stepped

forward. "Excuse me, Doctor," he said. "I understand the volunteer has an artificial limb." He turned to Barker. "If you'll please remove your trousers sir?"

Hawks smiled uncomfortably. "I'll hold your jacket," he said to Barker.

Barker looked around. Beads of cold moisture appeared on his forehead. He handed the windbreaker to Hawks without turning his face toward him, opened his belt and stepped out of the slacks. He stood with them clutched in his hands, looked at Hawks, then rolled them up quickly and put them down on the edge of the table.

"Now, if you'll just lie down in the suit, sir, we'll see what needs adjusting." The ensign gestured to his team and they closed in around Barker, lifting him up and putting him down on his back inside the opened suit. Barker lay rigid, staring up, and the ensign said, "Move yourself around, please—we want to make sure your muscles make firm contacts with all the servomotor pressure plates."

Barker began stiffly moving his body.

The ensign said, "Yes, I thought so. The artificial limb will have to be built up in the region of the calf, and on the knee joint. Fidanzato—" He gestured to one of his men. "Measure those clearances and then get down to the machine shop. I want some shim plates on there. I'm sorry, sir," he said to Barker, "but you'll have to let my man take the leg with him. It won't take long. Sampson—help this man off with his shirt so you can get at the shoulder strap."

Barker jerked his arms up out of the suit, grasped the edges of the torso backplate, and pulled himself up to a sitting position. "I'll take my own shirt off, sonny," he rasped, and pulled it off over his head. As Sampson unbuckled the leg's main strap, Barker looked twistedly at Hawks and ticked the edge of the armor shell with his fingers. "New artifices, Mage?" He seemed to be expecting some special response to this.

Hawks frowned. Barker's grin became even more distorted with irony. He looked around him. "Well, that's one flunk. Anybody else care to try? Maybe I should tie one hand behind my back, too?"

The ensign said uncertainly to Hawks, "It's a quotation from a play, Doctor." He looked at Barker, who solemnly wet a fingertip and described an X in the air.

"Score one for the NROTC graduate."

The other men in the dressing team kept their heads down and worked.

"What kind of a play, Ensign?" Hawks asked quietly.

"I read it in my English Lit course," the ensign said uncomfortably, flushing as Barker winked. "Merlin the Magician has made an invincible suit of armor. He intended it for Sir Galahad, but as he was making it, the needs of the magic formula forced him to fit it to Lancelot's proportions. And even though Lancelot has been betraying King Arthur, and they'll be fighting in the joust that day, Merlin can't let the armor just go unused. So he calls Lancelot into his workshop, and the first thing Lancelot says when he comes in and sees the magic armor is: 'What's this—new artifices, Mage?'"

Barker grinned briefly at the ensign and then at Hawks. "I hoped you'd recognize the parallel, Doctor. After all, you say you've read a book or two."

"I see," Hawks said. He looked thoughtfully at Barker, then asked the ensign, "What's Merlin's reply?"

"'Aye. Armorings.'"

Barker's mouth hooked upward in glee. He said to Hawks, "'Armorings? Sooth, Philosopher, you've come to crafting in your tremblant years? You've put gnarled fingers to the metal-beater's block, and hammered on Damascus plate to mime the armiger's employe?'"

The ensign, looking uncertainly from Hawks to Barker, quoted: "'How I have done is no concern for you. . . . Content yourself that when an eagle bends to make his nest, such nests are built as only eagles may inhabit. —Or those who have an eagle's leave.'"

Barker cocked an eyebrow. "'And I've your leave, old bird?'"

"'Leave and prayer, headbreaker,'" the ensign replied to him.

"'You like me not,'" Barker said, frowning at Hawks. "'And surely Arthur'd not command you to enwrap this body's hale and heart beyond all mortal damage. Nay, not this body—he's not fond of *my* health, eh?—Well, that's another matter. You say this armor comes from you? Then it *is* proof, weav'd up with your incantings? 'Tis wondrous strong? For me? As I began, you like me not—why is this, then? Who has commanded you?'"

The ensign licked his lips and looked anxiously at Hawks. "Should I go on, Doctor?"

Hawks smiled thinly at Barker. "Why, yes—let's see how it comes out. If I like the condensation, maybe I'll go out and buy the book."

"Yes, sir." The ensign's men had not looked up. Sampson

was fumbling absorbedly with the buckles of the shoulder strap.

"'My craft commands me, Knight. As yours does you, in sign that craft loves man full well as wisely as a woman will. Take it. Never has armor such as this bestrode a horse. Never so good a craftsman's eyes has measured out its joinings, or wrought so tenderly. Never have marker's eyes so earnestly conjoined with artificer's hands and engine-shaper's mind, as were met here to borrow from *your* thews that motive force which, in the sum, will take all glory. Take it—be damned to you! —take it, you that have overmastered more than is your measure, and seek to overmaster more!'"

"'There's a jealousy in you, old man,'" Barker said.

"'You know not what of!'"

"'You know, then, so surely, the things my silent mind wots? Be not so proud, Magician. 'Tis as you say—I, too, know what it is to be of craft. And I've my pride, as well as you have yours. Will it entail me glory, do you think, to take with your gift what I well might giftless gain?'"

"'You must!'"

"'Or where's your mageing? Aye—and what's my craft, to ware itself of yours? Take it I shall, though I misdoubt myself. You warrant it for proof? It will not fail, upon some field, against some lance unknown to your devising?'"

"'An it shall fail, then fail I with you, Knight.'"

Barker impatiently shrugged Sampson off and reached up to where the narrow band of leather had creased his shoulder permanently. He pulled it down and unbuckled the broad band across his stomach. "'Then fail not, Armiger,'" he whispered. "'I pray you—do not fail.'"

Hawks looked at Barker quietly for a moment. Then he wet a forefinger and described an X in the air. "Score one for the whole man," he said. As he said it, a flash of pain crossed his face.

3

Fidanzato walked away with Barker's leg. A technician came up to Hawks. "Your secretary's on the phone, Ed," he said. "Asked me to tell you it's urgent."

Hawks shook his head to himself. "Thanks," he said distractedly, and went across the laboratory to an isolated wall box. He picked up the extension handset. "This is Hawks, Vivian. What is it—a call from Tom Phillips? No, it's all right—I've been expecting it. I'll take it here." He held on, his eyes blank, waiting while the admiral's call was switched to the laboratory. Then the diaphragm in the earpiece rattled again, and he said, "Yes, Tom. Oh, I'm all right. Yes. Hot in Washington, is it? No, not here. Just smog. Well." He stood listening, and looking at the featureless wall before him.

"Yes," he said slowly. "Well, I rather thought the report on Rogan would have that effect. No, listen—we have a new approach. We've found a new man. I think he'll work out all right. No, look—I mean a new *kind* of man; I think we've got a good chance with him. No, no—listen, why don't you look up his record? Al Barker. Yes. Barker. There should be an Army 201 file from the Office of Strategic Services records. And an FBI security clearance. Yes. You see, the thing is, he's a completely different kind of organism from a nice, decent kid like Rogan. Yes, the records would show it. How about a personal interview, if you need it for a convincer with the Committee? No, I know they're upset about Rogan and the others, but maybe if you—"

His unoccupied left hand plucked blindly and persistently at one of the buttons of his smock.

"No, Tom—think. Think, now—Look, if this was just one more volunteer, what purpose would I think I was serving? No, he *is* different. Look, if you—All right, if there isn't time, there isn't time. When are they going to meet again? Well, it seems to me there's plenty of flying time between now and day after tomorrow. You could come out here and—"

He shook his head at the wall and put the flat of his palm up against it. "All right. I know you're a busy man. All right, then, if you're on my side and you don't need to fly out here because you trust me, why don't you trust me? I mean, if I think the next shot'll make it, why can't you take my word for it?"

He listened, and said peevishly: "Well, damn it, if the Committee won't make an official decision until day after tomorrow, why can't I go ahead until then? I'll have a successful shot on my record by then, we'll be rolling with this thing, we'll—Look—do you think I'd waste my *own* time if I didn't think this man could do it?"

He sighed, and said huskily, "Look, if I could *guarantee* what the results were going to be, I wouldn't need a research program! Let's try and do this thing step by step, if we're going to do it at all!"

He rubbed his hand over his face, pressing heavily against

it. "O.K., we're back to the same thing—what's the good of arguing? You'll give me money, rank, equipment, and everything, because it's me, but the first time it comes down to taking my word for something, nobody out there can get out of his half-assed panic long enough to think who they're dealing with. You think I'm doing all this by guesswork?"

He licked his lips and listened intently. Then he relaxed. "All right, then," he said with a wintry smile. "I'll call you early day after tomorrow and let you know the results. Yes, I'll remember the time difference! All right. And no, no—don't worry," he finished, "I'll give it the very best try I can. Yes. Well, you too, Tom. Be seeing you."

He racked the handset and turned away from it, his face drawn. He looked at his hands and put them in his pockets.

Sam Latourette had been waiting for him to finish. He came forward worriedly. "Trouble, Ed?"

Hawks grimaced. "Some. Tomorrow's shot has to make it."

"Or else?" Latourette asked incredulously. "Just like that? Years of work and millions of dollars, down the drain? Are they *crazy*?"

"No. No, they're human, Sam. It's beginning to look like good money after bad, to them. And men being lost. What do you want them to do? Go on feeling like accessories to senseless murder? And, after all—it's not as if the end of the Moon shots would be the end of the transmitter program, you know."

Latourette's face flushed. "Come off it, Ed! All that needs to happen is for the transmitter program to get one black eye like this, and even the company'll let it go. They'll pick it up again sometime, but not right away—and not with

you. You know that. They'll ease you out and close this
down until it's cooled off a little. They—"

"I know," Hawks said. "I've got too much of the smell
of death around me." He looked around. "But they won't
do it if Barker pays off for us, tomorrow. 'Success blinds
all.' Chaucer. Out of context." His face writhed into a twisted
smile. "The level of culture in this place is rising." He swung
his shoulders around, his face still contorted, like a child's
in the grip of unbearable frustration searching for the nursery
door. He said in a very low voice, "Sam, what a complicated
and terrible thing the human mind is!" He moved to begin
walking across the laboratory floor, his head down.

Latourette pawed clumsily at the air. "You can't *use*
Barker! You can't afford to get involved with someone as
wild and unpredictable as that! Ed, it won't *work*—it'll be
too much."

Hawks stopped still, his hands in his pockets, his eyes
shut. "Don't you think he'll work out?"

"Listen, if he has to be put up with day after day, it'll
get worse all the time!"

"So you do think he'll work out." Hawks turned and
looked at Latourette. "You're afraid he'll work out."

Latourette looked frightened. "Ed, he doesn't have sense
enough not to poke at every sore spot he finds in you. And
you're not the kind to ignore him. It'll get worse, and worse,
and you—"

"You said that, Sam," Hawks said gently. After a moment, he sent Latourette back to the transmitter, and once
again set out to walk across the laboratory toward Barker.

Hawks stood watching Barker's leg being refitted. Bulges

of freshly ground aluminum were bolted to the flesh-coloured material.

"Barker," he said at last, lifting his eyes to the man's face.

"Yes, Doctor?"

"We're pressed for time. I'd appreciate it if you went up and had our physician examine you now. As many of us as can be spared will take our lunch in the meantime."

"Doctor, you know damned well I passed an insurance physical last week."

"Last week . . ." Hawks said, looking down at the floor, "is not today. Tell Dr. Holiday I asked him to be as quick as he can and still be thorough. Try to return here as soon as he's finished." He turned away. "I'll be back in half an hour."

Hawks waited alone in Benton Cobey's reception room for twenty minutes, looking patiently down at his shoes. Finally the receptionist told him he could go in.

He crossed the bristly carpet, knocked once on the featureless mahogany sheet of Cobey's door, opened it and went through.

Continental's president sat behind a teak table that glowed with the oil of its dark, hand-rubbed finish, almost as black as bituminous coal. Cobey himself was a small, aggressive man with an undershot jaw and a narrow skull as bald as an egg. His deep tan had the faint tinge of a quartz lamp's work, and his lips were lightly blued by the first hint of cyanosis. His face had the pinched look of ulceration.

"All right, Ed," he said immediately. "What is it?"

Hawks pulled one of the over-comfortable armchairs away

from the side of the desk a little, and sat down, adjusting the crease in his trousers.

"Something wrong down in the lab, again?" Cobey asked.

"It's a personnel problem," Hawks said, looking over Cobey's left shoulder. "And I have to be back in the laboratory by one o'clock."

"See Connington about it."

"I don't know if he's in today. It's not in his province, in any case. What I want to do is make Ted Gersten my top assistant. He's qualified; he's been Sam Latourette's second for a year and a half. He can do Sam's job. But I need your authorization to do it by tomorrow. We're set up for a new shot then—the astronomical conditions are already past optimum; I want to get in as many shots as I can this month—and I want Sam off it by then." His right hand had unconsciously moved to the end of his tie. He clamped the end between his fore and middle fingers, and began working the point of the cloth in under his thumbnail.

Cobey leaned back and folded his hands. His knuckles became mottled with red. "Six months ago," he said in a low voice, "when I wanted to have Latourette sent home, you pulled that phony business of needing him to help set up your amplifier, or something."

Hawks took a breath. "Hughes Aircraft needs a project engineer on a short-term research program for the Army. Frank Waxted wants Sam on it, if he can get him. He can get a contingent approval from Hughes' personnel department."

Cobey sat forward. "Waxted wouldn't call you about Sam if he didn't have an idea he could get him. Look, Hawks," Cobey said, "I'll take a lot from you—even more than the

Navy makes me take. Don't kid yourself, if I didn't respect your brains, I'd have your hide any time I wanted it, and blow the contract; I'll still be here and the company'll still be here after this Moon business is over and done.

"Don't go pussyfooting around behind my back! Don't tell me about calls from Waxted when I'd lay dollars to dimes he doesn't know the first thing about it yet! I'm telling you, Hawks."

Hawks said, "I'm here. I'm telling you what I want. I've arranged the situation so all you have to do is make a yes or no decision."

"I always say you do neat work. What *is* this, Hawks? Why do you want Latourette off your hands?" Cobey's eyes narrowed. "Latourette's been your shadow ever since he came here. If I want ten minutes of lecture on the march of modern electronics, I ask Latourette how you've been feeling lately. What's the matter, Hawks—you and Sam have a falling out?"

Hawks had still not met Cobey's eyes from the moment he had entered the office.

"Relationships between people are a complicated thing." Hawks was speaking slowly and distinctly, as if he antici-pated a stoppage in his throat. "People lose control of their emotions. The more intelligent they are, the more subtly they do it. Intelligent men pride themselves on their control. They go to elaborate lengths to disguise their impulses— not from the world; they're not hypocrites—from them-selves. They find rational bases for emotional actions, and they present logical excuses for disaster. A man may begin a whole series of errors and pursue it to the brink of the pit, and over the brink, all unaware."

"What you mean is, you had some kind of set-to with Latourette. He wants to do one thing and you want to do another."

Hawks said doggedly, "People under emotional stress always resort to violence. Violence doesn't have to be a fired gun; it can be a slip of a pencil on a chart, or a minor decision that brings an entire program down. No supervisor can watch his assistants continually. If he could, he wouldn't need help on the job. As long as Latourette's on the project, I can't feel I'm in total control of things."

"And you have to have that? Total control?"

"I have to have that."

"So Latourette's got to go. Just like that. Six months ago, he had to stay. Just like that."

"He's the best man for the job. I know him better than I know Gersten. That's why I want Gersten now—he hasn't been my friend for ten years, the way Sam has."

Cobey caught his lower lip between his teeth and slowly pulled it free without relaxing the pressure. He leaned forward and tapped a memorandum pad with the end of his pen. "You know, Hawks," he said, "this can't go on. This began as a simple Navy research contract. All we were was the hardware supplier, even if you did initiate the deal. Then the government found that thing on the Moon, and then there was all that trouble, and suddenly we're not just working with a way to transmit people, we're operating as an actual installation, we're fooling around with telepathy, we've got men dead and men psychotic, and *you* are in it up to your ears.

"I came in here one morning, and found a letter on my desk informing me you're all at once a Navy commander and in charge of operating and maintaining the installation. Meaning you're in a position to demand from us, as a Naval officer, any equipment you, as one of our engineers, decide the installation needs. The Board of Directors won't tell me the basis for the funds they've allocated. The Navy tells me nothing. You're supposed to be a ConEl employee, and I don't even know where your authority stops—all I know is ConEl money is being spent against the day when the Navy might pay us back, if Congress doesn't cut the armed services budget so that they can't, under the terms of the research contract—which, for all I know, has been superseded under the terms of some obscure paragraph in the National Defense Acts. All I do know is that if I run Continental into the red so deep it can't get out, I'll be out on my ear for the stockholders to be happy over."

Hawks said nothing.

"You didn't make the system I've got to work with," Cobey said. "But you've sure as hell exploited it. I don't dare give you a direct order. I'm dead sure I couldn't fire you outright if I wanted to. But my job is running this company. If I decide I can't run it with you in it, and I can't fire you, I'm going to *have* to pull some dirty deal to force you out. Maybe I'll even make that nice little speech about emotional violence." He turned sharply and said, "*Look* at me, God damn you! *You're* making this mess—not me!"

Hawks stood up and turned away. He walked slowly toward Cobey's door. "Can I, or can I not release Sam to Waxted and promote Gersten?"

Cobey scrawled a note on his memory pad with jabbing strokes of his pen. "Yes!"

Hawks' shoulders slumped. "All right, then," he said, and closed the door behind him.

4

When he returned to the laboratory, Barker had been fitted with the first of his undersuits and was sitting on the edge of the dressing table, smoothing the porous silk over his skin, with talcum powder showing white at his wristlets and around the turtle neck. The undersuit was bright orange, and as Hawks came up to him Barker said, "I look like a circus acrobat."

Hawks looked at his wrist watch. "We'll be ready for the scan in about twenty minutes. I want to be with the transmitter test crew in five. Pay attention to what I'm going to tell you."

"Lunch disagree with you, Doctor?"

"Let's concentrate on our work. I want to tell you what's going to be done to you. I'll be back later to ask you if you want to go through with this, just before we start."

"That's very kind."

"It's necessary. Now, listen: the matter transmitter analyzes the structure of whatever is presented to its scanners. It converts that analysis into a signal, which describes the exact atomic structure of the scanned object. The signal is transmitted to a receiver. And, at the receiver, the signal is fed into a resolving stage. There the scanned atomic structure is duplicated from a local supply of atoms—half a ton of rock will do, and to spare. In other words, what the matter transmitter will do is to tear you down and then send a message to a receiver telling it how to put you together again.

"The process is painless and, as far as your consciousness is concerned, instantaneous. It takes place at the speed of light, and neither the electrochemical impulses which transmit messages along your nerves and between your brain cells, nor the individual particles constituting your atoms, nor the atoms in their individual movements, travel at quite that rate.

"Before you could possibly be conscious of pain or dissolution, and before your atomic structure could have time to drift out of alignment, it will seem to you as if you've stood still and the universe has moved. You'll suddenly be in the receiver, as though something omnipotent had moved its hand, and the electrical impulse that was a thought racing between your brain cells will complete its journey so smoothly that you will have real difficulty, for a moment, in realizing that you have moved at all. I'm not exaggerating, and I want you to remember it. It'll be important to you.

"Another thing to remember is that you won't actually have made the journey. The Barker who appears in the receiver has not one atom in his body that is an atom in your body now. A split second ago, these atoms were part of a mass of inorganic material lying near the receiver. The

Barker who appears was created by manipulating those atoms—stripping particles out of some, adding particles to others, like someone robbing Peter to pay Paul.

"It makes no functional difference—this is in theory, remember—that the Barker who appears is only an exact duplicate of the original. It's Barker's body, complete with brain cells duplicating the arrangement and electrical capacities of the originals. This new Barker has your memories, complete, and even the memory of the half-completed thought that he finishes as he stands there. But the original Barker is gone, forever, and his atoms have been converted into the energy that drove the transmitter."

"In other words," Barker said, "I'm dead." He shrugged his shoulders. "Well, that's what you promised me."

"No," Hawks said. "No," he repeated slowly, "that's not the thing I promised you. Theoretically, the Barker who appears in the receiver could not be distinguished from the original in any way. As I said in the beginning, it will seem to him that nothing has happened. When it happens to you, it'll seem to you that it's *you* who's standing there. The realization that somewhere else, once, there was a Barker who no longer exists, will be purely academic. You will know it because you'll remember my telling it to you now. You won't feel it.

"You'll have a clear memory of being put into the suit, of being wheeled into the transmitter, of feeling the chamber magnetic field suspending your suit with you inside it, of the lights being turned out, and of drifting down to the chamber floor and realizing you must be in the receiver. No, Barker," Hawks finished, nodding to the dressing team, which came forward with the cotton underwear and the rubberized pressure suit Barker would wear next to his armor. "When I kill you, it'll be in other ways. And you'll be able to feel it." He walked away.

He came up to where Sam Latourette was checking over the transmitter, and raised his arm, but stopped himself before putting it around the man's shoulders. "How's it going, Sam?" he asked.

Latourette looked around. "Well," he said slowly, "it's transmitting the test objects perfectly." He nodded toward the attendant cradling an anesthetised spider monkey in his arms. "And Jocko's been through the transmitter and out the receiver here five times. The scan checks perfectly with the tape we made on the first shot today, and within the statistical expectation of drift from yesterday's tape. It's the same old Jocko every time."

"We can't ask for more than that, can we?" Hawks said.

"No, we can't," Latourette said implacably. "It'll do the same for him." He jerked his head in the direction of the dressing table. "Don't worry."

"All right, Sam." Hawks sighed. "I wouldn't propose him for membership in a country club, either." He looked around. "Is Ted Gersten with the receiver crew?"

"He's up working on one of the signal modulation racks. It's the only one that didn't test out. He's having it torn down. Says he'll have it rewired tonight in plenty of time for tomorrow."

Hawks frowned thoughtfully. "I'd better go up there and talk to him. And I think he should be here with us when Barker goes in for the scan." He turned away, then looked back. "I wish you'd cycle Jocko through once more. Just to be sure."

Latourette's lips pinched together. He motioned to the monkey's attendant with a clawed sweep of his arm.

Gersten was a spare man with leathery features and deep, round eyesockets whose rims stood out clearly under his taut facial skin. His broad, thin lips were nearly the color of his face. When he spoke, they peeled back from his teeth to give an impression of great intensity. His voice, in contrast, was soft, deep, and low. He stood gently scratching his iron-gray hair, watching the two technicians who were lifting a component chassis out of its rack, which had been pulled out of the array and set down on the gallery floor.

The test-signal generator's leads dangled from the service rack overhead. Other pieces of test equipment were set down around the three men. As Hawks came walking up from the ladder at the end of the gallery, Gersten turned and watched him. "Hello, Ed."

"Ted." Hawks nodded and looked down at the work being done. "What's the problem?"

"Voltage divider. It's picked up some kind of intermittent. Tests out fine for a while, then gets itself balled up, and straightens out again."

"Uh-huh. Sam tells me you're O.K. otherwise."

"That's right."

"O.K. Listen, I'm going to need you on the transmitter with Sam and myself when we scan the new volunteer. Want to come with me now?"

Gersten glanced at the technicians. "Sure. The boys're doing fine." He stepped clear of the test instruments and walked down the gallery toward the ladder, beside Hawks.

When they were out of earshot of the technicians, Hawks said, casually, "You may have a lot to do tomorrow, Ted. No sense wasting time on a wiring job tonight, when you could be sleeping. Requisition a new divider from Manufacturing, messenger express delivery, and send the old one back to them. Let it be their headache. Either way, you'd have to run complete tests all over again anyhow."

Gersten blinked. "I should have looked at it that way myself, I think." He glanced at Hawks. "Yes. I should have." He stopped and said, "I'll be right down after you, Ed." He turned and walked back toward his technicians.

Hawks lowered himself down the iron ladder, his shoe soles tapping regularly and softly. He walked back across the laboratory floor, where Latourette was watching the instruments above the tape deck of a castered gray cabinet connected to a computer, and occasionally calling for the computer technician to read out his figures. The spider monkey was once again in the attendant's arms, stirring drowsily against his chest as the anesthetic wore off.

Hawks watched silently as Latourette compared the taped readings with the data being given to him by a technician from the receiver crew, who was operating another service computer.

"All right, Bill," Latourette said, turning away. "But let's run both sets together for comparison, now. Let me know if anything's off."

The technician nodded.

"Well," Latourette said to Hawks, "as far as I could tell

from the rough check, your friend Barker still has the equipment one hundred per cent behind him." He looked toward the spider monkey. "And Jocko certainly looks healthy enough." He turned back. "Where's Gersten?"

"He'll be right down." Hawks looked up at the galleries. "I wish I knew Gersten better. He's a hard man to understand. He never shows more than he has to. It's very hard to accommodate yourself to a man like that."

Latourette looked at him peculiarly.

5

Barker lay on the table, enclosed in the armor suit, with his faceplate open. He looked calmly up as Hawks bent over him.

"All right?" Hawks asked.

"Fine." Barker's voice echoed in the helmet and came distorted through the narrow opening. His air hoses lay coiled on his stomach.

The ensign, standing beside Hawks, said, "He seems to be quite comfortable. I don't think there'll be any trouble with claustrophobia. Of course, we won't know until we've closed his faceplate and had him breathing tanked air for a while."

"Son," Barker said, "I've dived more feet in my life than you've walked."

"This is hardly scuba gear, sir."

Hawks moved into the line of vision between Barker's face and the ensign's. He said, "Barker, I told you I was going to give you a chance to back out now, if you wanted to."

"I like the way you put that, Doctor."

"The reason we have all this elaborate control gear should be obvious," Hawks persisted. "The fidelity of the resolving process depends on the clarity of the signal that arrives at the receiver. And even the tightest beam we can drive up to the Moon is going to pick up a certain amount of noise. So we feed from the transmitter here to the amplifier banks, checking the signal against the readings we take on the first scan.

"There's always a variation between the file tape and the signal, of course. We make a new file tape with every transmission, but there's still a time lag between the making of the latest tape and the next transmission of the same object. But that's why we have a standard man, and a statistical table of the probable degree of variation over given periods of time. By setting up crude analogies in the amplifiers, and introducing the proper statistical factor, we can introduce a certain measure of control."

"I hope you think I'm following this, Hawks."

"I hope you try. Now. When we've done all this, we have as much accuracy as we can. At that point, the signal is pulsed up to the Moon, not once but repeatedly. Another differential amplifier bank in the receiver there compares each bit of information in each signal pulse to each bit of all the signals it has received. It rejects any bit which differs from a majority of its counterparts. Any error created by transmission noise is almost certain to be discarded in the process.

"What we're going to do today is scan you for the first

time. Nine-tenths of our control equipment is useless until it has scan readings to work from. So, the first time, you're trusting entirely to our ability as electronic engineers, and my skill as a designer. I can't guarantee that the Al Barker who is resolved in the laboratory receiver will be the same man you are now. You can test an electronic component until you're blue in the face, and have it fail at the most critical moment. The very process of testing it may have weakened it just enough. And the scanner itself represents a broad departure from the usual electronic techniques for which a broad base of familiar theory is available. I know how it works. But there are places where I don't yet know why. You have to realise— once the scan is in progress, we can't correct any errors the hardware may be making. We're blind. We don't *know* which bit of the signal describes which bit of the man. We may never know.

"When Thomas Edison spoke into the horn of his sound reproducer, the vibration of his voice against a diaphragm moved a needle linked to that diaphragm, and scratched a variable line on the rotating wax cylinder. When he played it back, out came 'Mary had a little lamb.' But there Edison was stopped. If the needle came loose, or the wax had a flaw, or the drive to the cylinder varied, out came something else—an unintelligible hash of noise.

"There was nothing Edison could do about it. He had no way of knowing what part of a scratch was song, and what was noise. He had no technique for taking a stylus in his hand and simply scratching a cylinder so that it could be played as 'Mary had a little lamb.' He could only check his reproducer for mechanical failure and begin, again, with his voice, and the horn, and the diaphragm. There was simply no other way for him to do it. And, of course, he needed none. There is no particularly great expenditure in saying 'Mary had a little lamb' over and over again as many times as it may take to get a perfect playback.

"And if Daguerre, experimenting with the beginnings of photography, found a plate overexposed or underexposed, or blotched by faulty chemicals or an imperfect lens, he could usually just try again. It didn't matter very much if, now and then, a picture was lost because the only way to save it would have been to know something that photography experts are only learning today.

"But we cannot do it, Barker. You are not 'Mary had a little lamb.' Nor are you a thing of light and shadow, to be preserved or lost at no critical expense to its source." Hawks smiled with wan self-consciousness. "A man is a phoenix, who must be reborn from his own ashes, for there is no other like him in the universe. If the wind stirs the ashes into a clumsy parody, then the phoenix is dead forever. Nothing we know of can bring you back.

"Understand me: the Al Barker we resolve will almost certainly be you. The statistical chances are all on your side. But the scanner can't discriminate. It's only a machine. A phonograph doesn't know what it's playing. A camera photographs everything it can see in front of it. It won't put in what isn't there, and it won't omit the lipstick smudge on your collar. But if, for some reason, the film has lost its red sensitivity, what comes up on the film doesn't look like lipstick at all—it might not look like anything. Do you understand what I'm trying to say? The equipment's set up as well as it can be. Once we have our negative, we get perfect prints every time. But it's the negative we're going after now."

Barker said lightly, "Ever had any trouble, Doctor?"

"If we have, we don't know it. As far as we could tell, our preliminary scans have all been perfect. At least, the objects and living organisms we've dealt with were able to go on functioning exactly as they always had. But a man is such a complex thing, Barker. A man is so much more than his gross physical structure. He has spent his life in thought—in filling his brain with the stored minutiae he remembers and reconnects when he thinks. His body is only a shell in which he lives. His brain is only a complex of stored memories. His mind—his mind is what he does with his memories. There is no other mind like it. In a sense, a man is his own creation.

"If we happen to change him on some gross level that can be checked against whatever is recorded of his life, we can detect that change. But we're not likely to be that far off. Far more serious is the possibility of there being enough error to cause subtle changes which no one could find— least of all you, because you'd have no data to check against. Was your first schoolbook covered in blue or red? If you remember it as red, who could find it now to see what color it was?"

"Does it matter?" Barker shrugged, and the suit groaned on the table. "I'd rather worry about the duplicate being so screwed up that it's dead, or turned into a monster that needs to die."

"Well," Hawks said, wiping his hand over his face, "that's not at all likely to happen. But you can worry about that if you want to. What you worry about depends entirely on where you draw the line on what parts of you are important to you. You have to decide how much of yourself can be changed before you consider yourself dead."

Barker smiled coldly up at him. He looked around at the encircling rim of the faceplate opening. "I'm in this thing now, Doctor. You know damned well I won't chicken out. I never would have. But you know you didn't do anything to help me."

"That's right, Barker," Hawks said. "And this is only a way in which I might kill you. There are other ways that are sure. I have to do this to you now because I need a man like you for what's going to be done to him later."

"Lots of luck, Doctor," Barker said.

The dressers had closed Barker's faceplate, and looped the air hoses back into connection with the tanks embedded in the armor's dorsal plate. A technician ran a radio check, and switched his receiver into the P.A. speaker mounted over the transmitter's portal. The sound of Barker's breath over the low-powered suit telephone began to hiss out regularly into the laboratory.

"We're going to wheel you in now, Barker," Hawks said into his microphone.

"Roger, Doctor."

"When you're in, we'll switch on the chamber electromagnets. You'll be held in mid-air, and we'll pull the table out. You won't be able to move, and don't try—you'll burn out the suit motors. You'll feel yourself jump a few inches into the air, and your suit will spread-eagle rigidly. That's the lateral magnetic field. You'll feel another jolt when we close the chamber door and the fore-and-aft magnets take hold."

"I read you loud and clear."

"We're simulating conditions for a Moon shot. I want you to be familiar with them. So we'll turn out the chamber lights. And there will be a trace component of formalin in your air to deaden your olfactory receptors."

"Uh-huh."

"Next, we'll throw the scanning process into operation. There is a thirty-second delay on that switch; the same impulse will first activate certain automatic functions of the suit. We're doing our best to eliminate human error, as you can see."

"I dig."

"A general anesthetic will be introduced into your air circulation. It will dull your nervous system without quite making you lose consciousness. It will numb your skin temperature-and-pressure receptors entirely. It will cycle out after you resolve in the receiver. All traces of anesthesia will be gone five minutes after you resolve."

"Got you."

"All right. Finally, I'm going to switch off my microphone. Unless there's an emergency, I won't switch it on again. And from this point on, my microphone switch controls the two servoactivated ear plugs in your helmet. You'll feel the plugs nudging your ears; I want you to move your head as much as necessary to allow them to seat firmly. They won't injure you, and they'll retract the instant I have emergency instructions to give you, if any. Your microphone will remain on, and we'll be able to hear you if you need any help, but you won't be able to hear yourself. All this is necessary on the Moon shots.

"You'll find that with your senses deadened or shut off, you'll soon begin to doubt you're alive. You'll have no way of proving to yourself that you're exposed to any external stimuli. You'll begin to wonder if you have a mind at all, any more. If this condition were to persist long enough, you would go into an uncontrollable panic. The required length of time varies from person to person. If yours exceeds the few minutes you'll be in the suit today, that'll be long enough. If it proves to be less than that, we'll hear you shouting, and I'll begin talking to you."

"That'll be a great comfort."

"It will."

"Anything else, Doctor?"

"No." He motioned to the Navy crew, and they began to roll the table into the chamber.

"I've got a word for the ensign," Barker said.

"All right."

The officer moved up into Barker's line of vision through the faceplate. He pantomimed "What?" with his mouth.

"The name is Barker, son. Al Barker. I'm not just another guinea pig for you to stuff into a tin can. You got a name, son?"

The ensign, his cheeks flushed, nodded.

"Be sure and tell me what it is when I come out of this, huh?"

Fidanzato, pushing at the foot of the table, chuckled very softly.

* * *

Hawks looked around. Latourette was at the transmitter control console. "Watch Sam," Hawks said to Gersten standing beside him, "and remember everything he does. Try not to miss anything." Hawks' eyes had not turned toward Gersten; his glance had swept undeviatingly over Weston, who was leaning back against an amplifier cabinet, his arms and ankles crossed, and over Holiday, the physician, standing tensely potbellied at the medical remote console.

Gersten grunted, "All right," and Hawks' eyes flickered with frustration.

The green bulb was still lighted over the transmitter portal, but the chamber door was dogged shut, trailing the cable that fed power to its share of the scanner components. The receiver chamber was sealed. The hiss of Barker's breath, calm but picking up speed, came from the speaker.

"Sam, give me test power," Hawks said. Latourette punched a console button, and Hawks glanced at the technicians clustered around the input of the amplifier bank. A fresh spool of tape lay in the output deck, its end threaded through the brake rollers and recording head to the empty takeup reel. Petwill, the engineer borrowed from Electronic Associates, nodded to Hawks.

"Sam, give me operating power," Hawks said. "Switch on." The lights over the transmitter and receiver portals leaped from the green bulbs into the red. Barker's breath sighed into near silence.

Hawks watched the clock mounted in the transmitter's face. Thirty seconds after he had called for power, the multichannel tape began to whine through the recording head, its reels blurred and roaring. A brown disc began to grow around the takeup spindle with fascinating speed. The green bulb over the receiver portal burst into life. The green bulb came back on over the transmitter.

The brakes locked on the tape deck. The takeup reel was three-quarters filled. Barker's shallow breath came panting through the speaker.

Hawks pressed his hand against the back of his bent neck and pulled it around across the taut muscle that corded down to his shoulder. "Doctor Holiday, any time you're ready to ease up on the anesthesia . . ."

Holiday nodded. He cranked the reduction-geared control wheel remote-linked to the tank of anesthetic gas in Barker's armor.

Barker's breathing grew stronger. It was still edging up toward panic, but he had not yet begun to mumble into his microphone.

"How does it sound to you, Weston?" Hawks asked.

The psychologist listened reflectively. "He's doing pretty well. And it sounds like panic breathing: no pain."

Hawks shifted his glance. "What about that, Doctor Holiday?"

The little man nodded. "Let's hear how he does with a little gas." He put his hands back on the controls.

Hawks thumbed his microphone switch. "Barker," he said gently.

The breathing in the speaker became stronger and calmer.

"Barker."

"Yes, Doctor," Barker's irritated voice said. "What's your trouble?"

"Doctor Hawks," Holiday said from the console, "he's down to zero anesthesia now."

Hawks nodded. "Barker, you're in the receiver. You'll be fully conscious almost immediately. Do you feel any pain?"

"No!" Barker snapped. "Are you all through playing games?"

"I'm turning the receiver chamber lights on now. Can you see them?"

"Yes!"

"Can you feel all of your body?"

"Fine, Doctor. Can you feel all of yours?"

"All right, Barker. We're going to take you out now."

The Navy crew began to push the table toward the receiver as Latourette cut the fore-and-aft magnets and technicians began undogging the chamber door. Weston and Holiday moved forward to begin examining Barker as soon as he was free of the suit.

Hawks said quietly to the ensign, "Be sure to tell him your name," as he walked to the control console. "All right, Sam," he said as he saw the table slip under Barker's armor, rising on its hydraulic legs to make contact with it. "You can slack down the primary magnets."

"You figure he's all right?" Latourette asked.

"I'll let Weston and Holiday tell me about it. He certainly sounded as if he's as functional as ever."

"That's not much," Latourette growled.

"It's—" Hawks took a deep breath and began again, gently. "It's what I need to do the job." He put his arm around Latourette's shoulders. "Come on, Sam, let's go for a walk," he said. "We'll have Weston's and Holiday's preliminary reports in a minute. Ted can start setting up for tomorrow's shot."

"I want to do it."

"No—No, you let him take care of it. It's all right. And—and you and I'll be able to go up and get out in the sunshine. There's something I have to tell you."

FOUR

Hawks sat with his back pressed into the angle of the couch in Elizabeth Cummings' studio. He held his brandy glass cupped loosely in his hands, and watched the night sky through the frames of glass behind her. She was curled in the window seat, her profile to him, her arms clasped around her drawn-up knees.

"My first week in high school," he said to her, "I had to make a choice. Did you go to grammar school here in the city?"

"Yes."

"I went to school in a very small town. The school was fairly well equipped—there were four rooms for less than seventy pupils. But there were only three teachers, including the principal, and each of them taught three grades, including pre-primary. It meant that, two-thirds of each day, my teachers were unavailable to me. They were there, teaching the other two grades things I either knew or wasn't expected to understand. Then when I went to high school, I suddenly found myself with a teacher for *each subject*. Toward the end of the first week, the high school principal and I happened to meet in the hall. She'd read my intelligence test results and things, and she asked me how I liked high school. I told her I was having a wonderful time." Hawks smiled down at his brandy glass. "She drew herself up and her face turned to stone. "You're not here to have fun!" she said, and marched away.

"So I had a choice. I could either find my school work a punishment, after that, and find ways to evade it, or I could *pretend* I felt that way about it, and use the advantages that pretence gives. I had a choice between honesty and dishonesty. I chose dishonesty. I became very grim, and marched to classes carrying a briefcase full of books and papers. I asked serious questions and mulled over my homework even in the subjects that bored me. I became an honor student. In a very little while, it *was* a punishment. But I had done it to myself, and I took the consequences of my dishonesty." He took a sip of brandy. "I wonder, sometimes, what I would have become if I'd chosen to go on the way I had been in grammar school—dipping into my teachers for whatever interested me, letting the rest of it slide, and continuing to enjoy my education."

He looked around. "This is a very nice studio you have here, Elizabeth. I'm glad I was able to see it. I wanted to see where you worked—what you did."

"Please go on telling me about yourself," she said from the window.

"I had only one other choice to make in high school," he said after a while in which he had simply sat and looked at her. "It was in my junior year, and I was about to take my first science subject. Physics. The physics teacher during my sophomore year had been a first-class man named Hazlet. His students nearly worshipped the ground he walked on. I had begun thinking by then in my life that going into the sciences was the answer for me.

"When I reported to class the first day of my junior year, I was full of anticipation. I had read a great deal of fiction about super-science and competent people doing competent things with it, and I expected more, I think, than even Hazlet could have crammed into a high-school physics class.

"But Hazlet wasn't there. I don't know what happened to him—went into government work, or, more likely, moved on to another school with a bigger budget. Whatever had happened, the school administration'd had to replace him. They had a woman teacher on their staff—a teachers'-college graduate, and all that, with all the necessary certificates—who had been hired to teach Spanish. She was a very gentle lady from the South, named Mrs. Cramer, with fine, delicate bones and pale features. Her skin was almost translucent, and her voice was perpetually breathless. While I was a sophomore, as I said, she'd been trying to teach Spanish grammar to a roomful of boys in patched bib overalls and farm work shoes. Just as everybody in the school knew about Hazlet, everybody also knew which side of Mrs. Cramer's desk had been in control of the class.

"So the next year, when I came into the physics lab, I found that Mrs. Cramer had been given a two-month summer education course in physics teaching, and had taken

Hazlet's place. It didn't work out very well. She had all sorts of teachers' guides to help her, and physics manuals detailing the classic formulae and problems. I imagine she went home every night and tried to memorize the next day's answers. But it just didn't work—she found that when she tried to do a blackboard problem for us as best she could, the result didn't agree with the answer she'd memorized. So she'd wipe out her answer and substitute the one in the manual, and tell us that even if she hadn't gotten the equations straight, this was the proper answer, and we should memorize it. When she gave tests, they never called for any problem calculations. They simply stated the problem and left a blank space for the proper answer.

"Even approaching it that way, she couldn't jam enough into her mind every night to cover all the necessary ground. She never learned, for example, that the chemical symbol for mercury wasn't *Mk*. It wasn't funny; it was pathetic. And she'd flare up into a gentlewomanly outrage whenever something went wrong, and sometimes she'd weep at her desk. I hope she found a job, somewhere—she wasn't back next year.

"But I had a choice. I had to decide whether I would join the class in staring out the window and tittering at Mrs. Cramer, or put in my time there each day, ignoring the whole business—it was either ignore it or burst into tears myself—and prowl through the public library for science texts to teach myself. It meant cutting myself off from the path the other individuals in the class were taking, and watching them lose themselves. I had a choice of staying with my own kind, or of being off by myself knowing I was swimming while they drowned.

"I chose to save myself. After a while, I began to reason that if they had embryo physicists among them, they'd straighten themselves out in college. I'd tried helping them with their work, some of them, until I realized they'd lost interest in understanding why the answers were what they were. If they really want to live, I said to myself, they'll find the energy to swim. If none of them swim, *ipso facto* none of them are really cut out to be scientists." He smiled with his eyes shadowed. "Life and science seem to have been equally important to me, when I was a boy. Nearly the same thing."

"And now?" Elizabeth asked.

"I'm not a boy any more. It isn't nineteen thirty-two."

"Is that your answer?"

"I can say the same thing with more words. I have work that has to be done by me, because I made it. I can't go back now and change the boy that I grew out of. I can see him; I can see his mistakes as well as his correct decisions. But I'm the man who grew out of the mistakes as well as out of the choices an adult would approve. I have to work with what I am. There's nothing else I can do—I can't forever sit in judgment on myself. A lump of carbon can't rearrange its own structure. It's either a diamond or a lump of coal—and it doesn't even know what coal or diamonds are. Someone else has to judge it."

They sat for a long time without speaking, Hawks with the empty brandy glass set on the coffee table beside his out-thrust legs, Elizabeth watching him from the window, the side of her face resting against her drawn-up knees.

"What were you thinking of now?" she asked when he stirred again and looked at his wrist watch. "Your work?"

"Now?" He smiled from a great distance. "No—I was thinking about something else. I was thinking about how X-ray photographs are taken."

"What about it?"

He shook his head. "It's complicated. When a physician X-rays a sick man, he gets a print showing the spots on his lungs, or the calcium in his arteries, or the tumour in his brain. But to cure the man, he can't take scissors and cut the blotch out of the print. He has to take his scalpel to the man, and before he can do that, he has to decide whether his knife could reach the disease without cutting through some part of the man that can't be cut. He has to decide whether his knife is sharp enough to dissect the malignancy out of the healthy tissue, or whether the man will simply re-grow his illness from the scraps left behind—whether he will have to be whittled at again and again. Whittling the X-ray print does nothing. It only leaves a hole in the celluloid. And even if there were some way to arrange the X-ray camera so that it would not photograph the malignancy, and if there were some way of bringing the X-ray print to life, the print still would have a hole through it to where the malignancy had been, just as if a surgeon had attacked it there with his scalpel. It would die of the wound.

"So what you would need is an X-ray film whose chemicals will not only *not* reproduce the malignancy but would reproduce healthy tissue, which they have never seen, in its place. You would need a camera that could intelligently rearrange the grains of silver on the film. And who could build such a camera? How am I to do that, Elizabeth? How am I going to build that sort of machine?"

*   *   *

She touched his hand at the door. His fingers quivered sharply. She said, "Please call me again as soon as you can."

"I don't know when that will be," he answered. "This— this project I'm on is going to take up a lot of time, if it works out."

"Call me when you can. If I'm not here, I'll be home."

"I'll call." He whispered, "Good night, Elizabeth." He was pressing his hand against the side of his leg. His arm began to tremble. He turned before she could touch him again and went quickly down the loft stairs to his car, the sound of his footsteps echoing clumsily downward.

FIVE

1

Hawks was sitting in his office the next morning when Barker knocked on the door and came in. "The guard at the gate told me to see you here," he said. His eyes measured Hawks' face. "Decided to fire me, or something?"

Hawks shook his head. He closed the topmost of the bundle of file folders on his desk and pointed toward the other chair. "Sit down, please. You have a great deal to think over before you go to the laboratory."

"Sure." Barker's expression relaxed. He walked over the uncarpeted floor with sharp scuffs of his jodhpur boot heels. "And by the way, good morning, Doctor," he said, sitting down and crossing his legs. The shim plate bulged starkly under the whipcord fabric stretched across his knee.

"Good morning," Hawks said shortly. He opened the file

and took out a large folded square of paper. He spread it out on his desk facing Barker.

Without looking at it, Barker said, "Claire wants to know what's going on."

"Did you tell her?"

"Did the FBI call me a fool?"

"Not in ways that concern them."

"I hope that's your answer. I was only reporting a fact you might be interested in." He smiled mirthlessly. "It cost me my night's sleep."

"Can you put in five minutes' maximum physical effort this afternoon?"

"I'd say so if I couldn't."

"All right, then. Five minutes is all you'll have. Now— this is where you're going." He touched the map. "This is the explored part of the far side of the Moon."

Barker frowned and leaned forward, looking down at the precisely etched hachurelines, the rectangle of territory bounded by lightly sketched areas marked: "No accurate data available."

"Rough country," he said. He looked up. "Explored?"

"Topographical survey. The Navy has an outpost located"—he put his finger down on a minute square—"there. Just over the edge of the visible disc at maximum libration. This"—he pointed to a slightly ragged circle a quarter inch away—"is where you're going."

Barker lifted one eyebrow. "What have the Russians got to say about all this?"

"This entire map," Hawks said patiently, "encompasses fifty square miles. The naval installation, and the place where you're going, are contained within an area half a mile square. They're almost the only unnatural formations at all visible from overhead. The others are the matter receiver beside the naval station and a relay tower near the edge of the visible disc. They're camouflaged—all but the place you're going, which can't be hidden. But the radiophotos from last month's Russian circumlunar rocket take in an area of at least seven million three hundred thousand square miles of lunar surface alone. Could you see a fly on the side of the Empire State Building's television tower? Through dirty glasses?"

"If I was up there with it."

"The Russians are not. We think they have a telemetering robot installation somewhere on the visible disk, and we expect them to rocket men up to it sometime next year. We haven't yet found it, but the statistical prediction locates their base about six thousand great circle miles from our installation. I don't feel we need worry about asking anyone's permission to go ahead with our program. However that may be, we are there, and this is where you're going today. . . . Now let me tell you how all this happened."

Barker leaned back in his chair, folded his arms, and arched his eyebrows. "I like your classroom manner," he murmured. "Have you ever considered a teaching career, Doctor?"

Hawks looked up at him. "I cannot let you die in ignorance," he finally said. "You're—you're free to leave this room at any time and terminate your employment here. Connington delivered your signed releases and contract to the company this morning. If you've read your contract, you'll remember the clause that permits you to cancel."

"Oh, I'll stick around, Doctor," Barker answered lightly.

"Thank you."

"You're welcome."

"Barker, you're not being easy on me at all, are you?"

"You're not doing so well by me, Doctor."

Hawks' right hand stirred the pile of folders, and he looked down at them. "You're right. Mercy is only a recent human cultural invention." He said in an overprecise tone, "Let's get to work. Earlier this year, the Air Force obtained one radioed photograph from a rocket which it attempted to put into a lunar orbit. The rocket came much too close, and crashed somewhere beyond the edge of the visible disk. By fortunate accident, that one photograph showed this." He took an eight-by-ten glossy print enlargement out of its folder and passed it to Barker. "You can see it's almost hopelessly washed out and striated by errors in transmission from the rocket's radiophoto sending apparatus. But this area, of which a part is visible in this corner—here—is clearly not a natural formation."

Barker frowned at it. "This what you showed me that ground photo of?"

"But that came a great deal later. All this showed was that there was something on the Moon whose extent and nature were not determined by the photograph, but which resembled no lunar or terrestrial feature familiar to human knowledge. We have, since then, measured its extent as best we can, and can say it is roughly a hundred meters in diameter and twenty meters high, with irregularities and amorphous features we cannot accurately describe. We still know very little of its nature—but that's beside the immediate point. When this feature was discovered, it became important to the government that it be studied. It had been pretty much expected that the far side of the Moon would show nothing startlingly different from the visible disk. Considering the unequal state of Russian and U.S. rocketry, it was now clear that if we did not move rapidly, the Russians had every chance of making a first-class discovery, whose nature we could not guess but whose importance might well be major—perhaps even decisive, as far as control of the Moon was concerned."

Hawks rubbed his eyes. "As it happened," he went on softly, "the Navy had some years previously signed a development contract with Continental Electronics, underwriting my work with the matter scanner. By the time of the Moon-photo rocket, the experimental system you see down in the laboratory had been built and despite its glaring crudities, had reached the point where it would consistently transmit a volunteer from the transmitter into the laboratory receiver without apparent damage. So, at a time when we were thinking of beginning experimental wireless transmission to a receiver in the Sierras, the government instituted a crash program to send volunteers to the Moon.

"A great deal of additional money was expended for equipment and personnel and, after a series of failures and near-misses, the Army rocket team was able to drop a relay tower on this side of the Moon's disk, near the edge. Then a very sketchy receiver was dropped, rather haphazardly, near this"—he tapped the chart frustratedly—"this formation. And a volunteer technician was broadcast through the relay tower into the receiver, which was barely large enough to hold him. Once there, he was supplied through the receiver. He was able to reach the rocket containing the relay tower, set it firmly on a stable base, and erect a plastic camouflage and meteorite impact-absorption hood over it. Using parts which were transmitted to him, he then built the receiver and return transmitter we are using now. He also erected rudimentary living quarters for himself, and then, apparently, began investigating the unknown formation against orders without waiting for the arrival of the Navy specialists who now crew the outpost.

"He wasn't found until several weeks ago. His was the second photograph I showed you. His body was inside the thing, and looked to the autopsy surgeons as though he had fallen from a height of several thousand meters under Terrestrial gravity."

Barker's mouth hooked briefly. "Could that have happened?"

"No."

"I see."

"*I* can't see, Barker, and neither can anyone else. We don't even know what to call that place. The eye won't follow it, and photographs convey only the most fragile impression. There is reason to suspect it exists in more than three spatial dimensions. Nobody knows what it is, why it's located there, what its true purpose might be, or what created it. We don't know whether it's animal, vegetable, or mineral. We know, from the geology of several meteorite craters that have heaped rubble against its sides, that it's been there for, at the very least, a million years. And we know what it does now: it kills people."

"Again and again, in unbelievable ways, Doctor?"

"Characteristically and persistently, in unbelievable ways. We need to know every one of them. We need to determine with no margin for error or omission, exactly what the formation can do to men. We need to have a complete guide to its limits and capabilities. When we have that, we can, at last, risk entering it with trained technicians who will study and disassemble it. It will be the technical teams which will actually learn from it as much as human beings can, and convey this host of information into the general body of human knowledge. But this is only what technicians always do. First we must have our chartmaker. It's my direct responsibility that the formation will, I hope, kill you again and again."

"Well, that's a fair warning even if it makes no sense. I can't say you didn't give it to me."

"It wasn't a warning," Hawks said. "It was a promise."

Barker shrugged. "Call it whatever you want to."

"I don't often choose my words on that basis," Hawks said.

Barker grinned at him. "You and Sam Latourette ought to do a brother act."

Hawks looked carefully at Barker for a long time. "Thank you for giving me something else to worry about." He picked up another folder and thrust it into Barker's hands.

"Look those over." He stood up. "There's only one entrance into the thing. Somehow, our first technician found it, probably by fumbling around the periphery until he stepped through it. It is not an opening in any describable sense; it is a place where the nature of this formation permits entrance by a human being, either by design or accident. It cannot be explained in more precise terms, and it can't be encompassed by the eye or, we suspect, the human brain. Three men died to make the chart which now permits other men, who follow the chart by dead reckoning like navigators in an impenetrable fog, to enter the formation. Other men have died to tell us the following things about its interior:

"A man inside it can be seen, very dimly, if we know where to look. No one knows, except in the most incoherent terms, what he sees. No one has ever come out; no one has ever been able to find an exit; the entrance cannot be used for that purpose. Non-living matter, such as a photograph or a corpse, can be passed out from inside. But the act of passing it out is invariably fatal to the man doing it. That photo of the first volunteer's body cost another man's life. The formation also does not permit electrical signals from its interior. That includes a man's speaking intelligibly inside his helmet, loudly enough for his RT microphone to pick it up. Coughs, grunts, other non-informative mouth-noises, are permissible. An attempt to encode a message in this manner failed.

"You will not be able to maintain communication, either by broadcast or along a cable. You will be able to make very limited hand signals to observers from the outpost, and you will make written notes on a tablet tied to a cord, which the observer team will attempt to draw back after you die. If that fails, the man on the next try will have to go in and pass the tablet out by hand, if he can, and if it is decipherable. Otherwise, he will attempt to repeat whatever actions you took, making notes, until he finds the one that killed you. We have a chart of safe postures and motions which have been established in this manner, as well as of fatal ones. It is, for example, fatal to kneel on one knee while facing lunar north. It is fatal to raise the left hand above shoulder height while in any position whatsoever. It is fatal past a certain point to wear armor whose air hoses loop over the shoulders. It is fatal past another point to wear armor whose air tanks feed directly into the suit without the use of hoses at all. It is crippling to wear armor whose dimensions vary greatly from the ones we are using now. It is fatal to use the hand motions required to write the English word 'yes,' with either the left or right hand.

"We don't know why. We only know what a man can and cannot do while within that part of the formation which has been explored. Thus far, we have a charted safe path and safe motions to a distance of some twelve meters. The survival time for a man within the formation is now up to three minutes, fifty-two seconds.

"Study your charts, Barker. You'll have them with you when you go, but we can't know that having them won't prove fatal past the point they measure now. You can sit here and memorize them. If you have any other questions, look through these report transcriptions, here, for the answers. I'll tell you whatever else you need to know when you come down to the laboratory. I'll expect you there in an hour. Sit at my desk," Hawks finished, walking quickly toward the door. "There's an excellent reading light."

2

Hawks was looking at the astronomical data from Mount Wilson, talking it over with the antenna crew, when Barker finally came through the double doors from the stairwell, holding the formation-chart folder. He was walking quickly and precisely, his face tight.

"All right, Will," Hawks said, turning away from the engineer in charge of the antenna. "You'd better start tracking the relay tower in twenty minutes. As soon as we've got him suited up, we'll shoot."

Will Martin nodded and took off his reading glasses to point casually toward Barker. "Think he'll chicken out?"

Hawks shook his head. "Especially not if it's put that way. And I've done that."

Martin grinned softly. "Hell of a way for him to make a buck."

"He can buy and sell the two of us a hundred times over, Will, and never miss an extra piece of pie out of his lunch money."

Martin looked at Barker again. "Why's he in this?"

"Because of the way he is." He began to walk toward Barker. "And, I suppose, because of the way I am. And because of the way that woman is," he murmured to himself. "I imagine we can mix Connington in, too. All of us are looking for something we must have if we're to be happy. I wonder what we'll get?"

"Now, look," Barker said, slapping the folder. "According to this, if I make a wrong move, they'll find me with all my blood in a puddle outside my armor, and not a mark on me. If I make another move, I'll be paralyzed from the waist down, which means I have to crawl on my belly. But crawling on your belly somehow makes things happen so you get squashed up into your helmet. And it goes on in that cheerful vein all the way. If I don't watch my step as carefully as a tightrope walker, and if I don't move on time and in position, like a ballet dancer, I'll never even get as far as this chart reads. I'd say I had no chance whatsoever of getting out alive."

"Even if you stood and did nothing," Hawks agreed, "the formation would kill you at the end of two hundred and thirty-two seconds. It will permit no man to live in it longer than some man has forced it to. The limit will go up as you progress. Why its nature is such that it yields to human endeavor, we don't know. It's entirely likely that this is only a coincidental side-effect of its true purpose—if it has one.

"Perhaps it's the alien equivalent of a discarded tomato can. Does a beetle know why it can enter the can only from one end as it lies across the trail to the beetle's burrow? Does the beetle understand why it is harder to climb to the left or right, inside the can, than it is to follow a straight line? Would the beetle be a fool to assume the human race put the can there to torment it—or an egomaniac to believe the can was manufactured only to mystify it? It would be best for the beetle to study the can in terms of the can's logic, to the limit of the beetle's ability. In that way, at least, the beetle can proceed intelligently. It may even grasp some hint of the can's maker. Any other approach is either folly or madness."

Barker looked up at Hawks impatiently. "Horse manure. Is the beetle happier? Does it get anything? Does it escape anything? Do other beetles understand what it's doing, and take up a collection to support it while it wastes time? A smart beetle walks around your tomato can, Doctor, and lives its life contented."

"Certainly," Hawks said. "Go ahead. Leave now."

"I wasn't talking about me! I was talking about you." Barker looked around the laboratory. He stared up at the instrument galleries. "Lot of people here. All because of you. I guess that feels pretty satisfying." He put the folder under one arm and stood with his hands in his pockets, his head to one side as he spoke flatly up into Hawks' face. "Men, money, energy—all devoted to the eminent Dr. Hawks and his preoccupations. Sounds to me like other beetles *have* taken up a collection."

"Looking at it that way," Hawks said dispassionately, "does keep it simple. And it explains why I continue to send men into the formation. It satisfies my ego to see men die at my command. Now it's your turn. Come on, Lancelot—your armor's waiting for you. Can't you hear the trumpet blowing? What's this—" He touched a lipstick smudge around a purple bruise on the side of Barker's neck. "A lady's favor? Whose heart will break if you should be unhorsed today?"

Barker knocked his hand away. "A beetle's heart, Doctor." His trained face fell into a ghastly, reminiscent smile. "A beetle's cold, cold heart."

Barker lay in his suit, his arms sprawled at his sides. Hawks had asked the Navy crew to step away from the table. Now he said softly, "You'll die, Barker. I want you to give up all hope. There isn't any."

"I know that, Doctor," Barker said.

"I've said you'd die again and again. You will. Today is only the first time. If you retain your sanity, you'll be all right—except you'll have the memory of dying, and the knowledge that you must die again tomorrow."

"In some other unbelievable way. You've told me this before." Barker sighed. "All right, Doctor—how are you going to do it? What little piece of magic are you going to work?" He was noticeably calm; in the same way he had faced Sam Latourette. His expression was almost apathetic. Only the black eyes, their pupils dilated broadly, lived in his face.

"There are going to be two of you," Hawks said. "When you're scanned, the signal describing you will be sent not only to the receiver on the Moon but to the one in the laboratory here. The signal to the laboratory receiver will be held in a tape delay deck until the duplicate signal has reached the Moon. Then both receivers will simultaneously resolve a Barker. We put this system into operation as soon as we understood there was no hope for the volunteer on the Moon. It means that, as far as Earth is concerned, the volunteer has not died. It has worked perfectly each time."

Barker looked patiently up at him.

Hawks went on laboriously. "It was conceived of as a lifesaving thing," he said, his upper lip twitching. "And it will save your life. Barker M, on the Moon, will die. But Barker L, here, will be taken out of his suit, and will be you, and will, if he retains his ability to remember coherently, and to reason, go home tonight as though this had been just another day in his life. And only *you*," he said, his stare focusing behind the surface of Barker's skull, "who stand on the Moon and remember me speaking to you now, will know that you are the luckless one, Barker M, and that a stranger has taken your place in the world."

His eyes returned to the Barker lying in the suit. "Someone else will hold Claire in his arms tonight. Someone else will drive your car and drink your whisky. You are not the Barker I met in your house. That man is gone. But no Barker has known death yet—no Barker has had to go into a place from which there is no return. You can get out of that suit at this moment, Barker, and leave here. I would." He watched the man intently.

After a moment, Barker's mouth opened into a deadly, silent laugh. "Come *on*, Doctor," he said. "Not when I can already hear the music."

Hawks pulled his hands out of sight behind his back. "All right. Then there is one last thing. When we began using this technique, we discovered that the L volunteer showed signs of momentary confusion. He behaved, even though safe in the laboratory, as if he were the M volunteer on the Moon. This confused period lasted only a moment or two, and swiftly waned into awareness. We put the phenomenon aside as one of the many things we must neglect now and reserve for study when the urgent problems have been solved. Many things have been put aside in that manner. But we received reports from the Navy crew Moonside that the M volunteer was unaccountably losing time—that he was disoriented for several seconds after he resolved in the receiver. Perhaps from brain damage, perhaps from something else—we did not know, at the time, but it was something new, and it was losing effective time for the volunteer.

"That was an urgent problem. We solved it when we considered the fact that for the first time in the universe as we know it, two *identical* brains existed in it, and at the same moment of time. It became apparent to us—unwilling though some of us were to accept the conclusion—that the quarter-million-mile distance separating them was no more important an impedance to their thoughts than a line scratched across his path is to a journeying man. You can call it anything you like. Telepathy if you want to, however you may feel about what is to be included in scientific nomenclature, and what is not." There was a momentary look of faint distaste on his face.

"It had no chance to be true communication, of course. Almost instantly, the two brains ceased being identical. The two volunteers were receiving vastly different sensory impressions and recording them in their individual brain cells. In seconds, the two minds were far apart, and the thread, frayed, came unravelled and broke. M and L were no longer the same man. And never, even at the first instant, could they simply 'speak' to each other in the sense of passing messages back and forth like telegrams. Nor, it seems to me, will that sort of objective, uninvolved communication ever be possible. To be able to read a man's mind is to be able to *be* that man—to be where he is, to live whatever he is living. Even in this special case of ours, the two men could only, for one decaying moment, seem to be of one mind."

Hawks looked around the laboratory. Gersten was watching him patiently, but standing idle, his preparations done. Hawks nodded absently, and looked back at Barker.

"We saw," he finished, "that we had here a potential means of accurately observing a man inside the lunar formation. So that is why we set up the physical circumstances of the Moon shots as we do. Barker M will resolve on the Moon, where the sensory-blocking devices in his armor will stop operating because they are out of range of our low-power controls here. He will come out of anesthesia and be able to move and observe normally. But Barker L, here, will still be under our control. He will be receiving no outside stimuli as he lies cut off inside his armor. His mind will be free of the environment of this laboratory, accepting whatever comes to it. And only what is in Barker M's mind can come to it.

"Barker L, too, will seem to himself to be on the Moon, inside the formation. He won't know he is Barker L. He will live as though in the M brain, and his organic structure will record whatever sensory perceptions the M body conveys to its brain. And though, of course, no method could prevent an eventual increep of divergent stimuli—the metabolic conditions of the two bodies gradually become less and less similar, for example—still the contact might last for as long as ten or fifteen minutes. But, of course, it never has.

"You'll know you've reached the limit of our previous probes when you reach Rogan's body. We don't know what killed him. It hardly matters what it was, except that you'll have to evade it, whatever it was. Maybe the condition of the body will be a useful clue. If it is, it'll be the only useful thing we've been able to learn from Rogan. Because when Rogan L, down here, felt Rogan M die, up there, Rogan L could not feel anything except Rogan M's death. The same thing will happen to you.

"Barker M's mind will die with his body, in whatever particular way the body is destroyed. Let's hope this happens at the end of a little more than two hundred and thirty-two seconds elapsed time, rather than less. It's bound to happen sooner or later. And Barker L's mind, safe down here in the L brain, will nevertheless *feel* itself die, because it isn't free to feel anything of what is happening to its own body. All its life, all its memories, will suddenly culminate. It will feel the pain, the shock, the as yet totally indescribable anguish of the end of its world. No man has been able to endure it. We found the finest, most stable minds we could among physically suitable volunteers, and without exception, all the L volunteers were taken out of their suits insane. Whatever information they had to give us was lost beyond all hope, and we gained nothing for our expenditure."

Barker stared flatly up at him. "That's too bad."

"How do you want me to talk about it?" Hawks answered rapidly. A vein bulged down the center of his forehead. "Do you want me to talk about what we're here to do, or do you want me to say something else? Are you going to argue morality with me? Are you going to say that, duplicate man or no duplicate man, a man dies on the Moon and makes me no less a murderer? Do you want to take me to court and from there to a gas chamber? Do you want to look in the law books and see what penalties apply to the repeated crime of systematically driving men insane? Will that help us here? Will it smooth the way?

"Go to the Moon, Barker. Die. And if you do, in fact, find that you love Death as feverishly as you've courted her, then, just perhaps, you'll be the first man to come back in condition to claim revenge on me!" He clutched the edge of the opened chest plate and slammed it shut. He held himself up with the flats of his palms on it and leaned down

until his face was directly over Barker's faceplate opening.
"But before you do, you'll tell me how I can usefully do it
to you again."

3

The Navy crew pushed Barker into the transmitter. The
lateral magnets lifted him off the table, and it was pulled
out from beneath him. The door was dogged shut, and the
fore-and-aft magnets came on to hold him locked immobile
for the scanner. Hawks nodded to Gersten, and Gersten
punched the Standby button on his console.

Up on the roof, there was a radar dish focused in parallel
with the transmitter antenna. Down in the laboratory, Will
Martin pointed a finger at the Signal Corps technician. A
radar beep travelled to the Moon and returned. The elapsed
time and Doppler progression were fed as data into a computer which set the precise holding time in the delay deck.
The matter transmitter antenna fired a UHF pulse through
the Moon relay tower into the receiver there, tripping its
safety lock so that it would accept the M signal.

Gersten looked at his console, turned to Hawks and said,
"Green board."

Hawks said, "Shoot."

The red light went on over the transmitter portal, and
the new file tape began roaring into the takeup pulleys of
the delay deck. One and a quarter seconds later, the leader
of the tape began to pass through the playback head feeding

the L signal to the laboratory receiver. The first hard beat of the M signal simultaneously reached the Moon.

The end of the tape clattered into the takeup reel. The green light lit over the laboratory receiver's portal. Barker L's excited breathing came through the P.A. speaker, and he said, "I'm here, Doctor."

Hawks stood in the middle of the floor with his hands in his pockets, his head cocked to one side, his eyes vacant.

After a time, Barker L said peevishly in a voice distorted by his numb lips, "All right, all right, you Navy bastards, I'm *goin'* in!" He muttered, "Won't even talk to me, but they're sure great at moving a man along."

"Shut up, Barker," Hawks said urgently under his breath.

"Going in now, Doctor," Barker said clearly. His breathing cycle changed. Once or twice after that, he grunted, and once he made an unconscious, high, keening noise of strain in his throat.

Gersten touched Hawks' arm and nodded toward the stopwatch in his hand. It showed two hundred and forty seconds of elapsed time since Barker had gone into the formation. Hawks nodded a nearly imperceptible reply. Gersten saw he was not moving his eyes away, and continued to hold the watch up.

Barker screamed. Hawks' body jumped in reflex, and his flailing arm sent the watch cartwheeling out of Gersten's hand.

Holiday, at the medical console, brought his palm down flat against a switch stud. Adrenalin fired into Barker L's heart as the anesthesia cut off.

"Get him out!" Weston was shouting. "Get him out!"

"There's no hurry any longer," Hawks said softly, as if the psychologist were standing where he could hear him. "Whatever was going to happen to him has happened."

Gersten looked toward the shattered watch and back at Hawks. "That's what I was thinking," he said.

Hawks frowned and began to walk toward the receiver chamber as the dressing crew pushed the armor table through the portal.

Barker sat hunched on the edge of the table, the opened armor lying dismembered beside him, and wiped his gray face. Holiday was listening to his heartbeat with a stethoscope, looking aside periodically to take a new blood-pressure reading as he squeezed the manometer bulb he kept in his hand. Barker sighed. "If there's any doubt, just ask me if I'm alive. If you hear an answer, you'll know." He looked wearily over Holiday's shoulder as the physician ignored him, and he said to Hawks, "Well?"

Hawks glanced at Weston, who nodded imperturbably. "He's made it, Dr. Hawks," Weston said. "After all, many neurotic personality constellations have often proved useful on a functional level."

"Barker," Hawks said, "I'm—"

"Yes, I know. You're happy everything worked out all right." He looked around. His eyes were darting in jerks from side to side. "So am I. Has somebody here got a cigarette?"

"Not yet," Holiday said sharply. "If you don't mind, chum, we'll leave your capillaries at normal dilation for a while, yet."

"Everyone's so tough," Barker mused. "Everyone knows

what's best." He looked around again at the laboratory people crowding around the table. "Could some of you stare at me a little later, please?" They retreated indecisively, then moved back to work.

"Barker," Hawks said gently, "do you feel all right?"

Barker looked at him expressionlessly. "I got up there, and out of the receiver, and started looking around the outpost. A bunch of zombies in light Navy suits handled me like you'd handle an ugly ghost. They wouldn't say two words to me without sounding as if they were paying for them. They showed me that camouflaged walkway they've built from the outpost bubble, and half-pushed me onto it. One of them walked along with me until I got to the formation, and never looked me in the face."

"They have problems of their own," Hawks said.

"I'm sure they do. Anyway, I got into the thing all right, and I moved along O.K. . . . It's—" His face forgot its annoyance, and his expression now was one of closely remembered bafflement. "It's—a little like a dream, you know? Not a nightmare, now—it's not all full of screams and faces, or anything like that—but it's . . . well, *rules*, and the crazy logic: Alice in Wonderland with teeth." He gestured as though quickly wiping his clumsy words from a blackboard. "I'll have to find ways of getting it into English, I guess. Shouldn't be too much trouble. Just give me time to settle down."

Hawks nodded. "Don't worry. We have a good deal of time, now."

Barker grinned up at him with a sudden flash of boyishness. "I got quite a distance beyond Rogan M's body, you know. What finally got me was—was—was the—was—"

Barker's face began to flush crimson, and his eyes bulged whitely. His lips fluttered. "The—the—" He stared at Hawks. "I can't!" he cried out. "I can't—Hawks—" He struggled against Holiday and Weston, who were trying to hold his shoulders, and curled his hands rigidly on the edge of the table, his arms locked taut, quivering in spasms. "Hawks!" he shouted as though from behind a thick glass wall. "Hawks, it didn't care! I was *nothing* to it! I was—I was—" His mouth locked partly open and the tip of his tongue fluttered against the backs of his upper teeth. "N-n-n . . . No—*N-nothing*!" He searched Hawks' face, desperate. He breathed as though there could never be enough air for him.

Weston was grunting with the effort to force Barker over backward and make him lie down. Holiday was swearing as he precisely and steadily pushed the needle of a hypodermic through the diaphragm of an ampule he had plucked out of his bag.

Hawks clenched his fists at his sides. "Barker! What color was your first schoolbook?"

Barker's arms loosened slightly. His head lost its rigid forward thrust. He shook his head and scowled down at the floor, concentrating fiercely.

"I—I don't remember, Hawks," he stammered. "Green—no, no, it was orange, with blue printing, and it had a story in it about three goldfish who climbed out of their bowl onto a bookcase and then dived back into it. I—I can see the page with the illustration: three fish in the air, falling in a slanted tier, with the bowl waiting for them. The text was set with three one-word paragraphs: 'Splash!', and then a paragraph indentation, and then 'Splash!' and then once more. Three Splashes in a tier, just like the fish."

"Well, now, you see, Barker," Hawks said softly. "You have been alive for as long as you can remember. You *are* something. You've seen, and remembered."

Weston looked over his shoulder. "For Heaven's sake, Hawks! Stay out of this!" Holiday studied Barker with a slight blinking of his eyes, the hypodermic withheld.

Hawks let out his breath slowly and said to Weston, "At least he knows he's alive."

Barker was slumped, now. Nearly doubled over, he swayed on the edge of the table, the color of his face gradually returning to normal. He whispered intently, "Thanks. Thanks, Hawks." Bitterly, he whispered, "Thanks for everything." He mumbled suddenly, his torso rigid, "Somebody get me a wastebasket, or something."

Gersten and Hawks stood beside the transmitter, watching Barker come unsteadily back from the washroom, dressed in his slacks and shirt.

"What do you think, Ed?" Gersten asked. "What's he going to do now? Is he going to pull out on us?"

"I don't know," Hawks answered absently, watching Barker. "I thought he'd work out," he said under his breath. "But has he?" He said to Gersten, "We'll simply have to wait and see. We'll have to think of a way to handle it."

"Get another man?"

Hawks shook his head. "We can't. We don't even know enough about this one." He said as though attacked by flies,

"I have to have time to think. Why does time run on while a man thinks?"

Barker came up to them.

Barker's eyes were sunken in their sockets. He looked piercingly at Hawks. His voice was jagged and nasal.

"Holiday says I'm generally all right, now, everything considered. But someone must drive me home." His mouth curled. "D'you want the job, Hawks?"

"Yes, I do." Hawks took off his smock and laid it folded atop the cabinet. "You might as well set up for another shot tomorrow, Ted," he said to Gersten.

"Don't count on me for it!" Barker sawed.

"We can always cancel, you know." He said to Gersten, "I'll call early tomorrow and let you know."

Barker stumbled forward as Hawks fell into step beside him. They slowly crossed the laboratory floor and went out through the stairwell doors, side by side.

Connington was waiting for them in the upstairs hall, lounging in one of the bright orange plastic-upholstered armchairs that lined the foyer wall. His legs were stretched out in front of him, and one hand held a cigar in front of his face as he lit it and blew smoke out of his pursed lips in a translucent cone. His eyes flicked once over Barker, and once over Hawks. "Have some trouble?" he asked as they came abreast of him. "I hear you had some trouble down in the lab," he repeated, his eyes glinting. "Rough time, Al?"

Hawks said, "If I find the man who's piping you information from the laboratory, I'll fire him."

Connington reached toward the standing ash tray beside

him. A ring on one finger clinked softly against the metal of the carrying handle. "You're losing your edge, Hawks," he said. "A couple of days ago, you wouldn't have bothered threatening." He pushed himself up to his feet, grunting softly as he said, "My doings would've been beneath you." He rocked up on his toes and back down on his heels, his hands in his pockets. "What's it matter, how many details I learn or don't? You think I need to? I know you two. That's enough."

"God damn you, Connington . . ." Barker began with the high, tearing note in his voice.

Connington's glance uppercut him lightly. "So I was right." He grinned consciously. "Goin' back to Claire, now?" He blew out smoke. "The two of you?"

"Something like that," Hawks said.

Connington scratched the lapel of his jacket. "Think I'll come along and watch." He smiled fondly at Barker, his head to one side. "Why not, Al? You might as well have the company of *all* the people who're trying to kill you."

Hawks looked at Barker. The man's hands fumbled as though dealing with something invisible in the air just in front of his stomach. He was staring right through Connington, and the personnel man squinted momentarily.

Then Barker said lamely, "There isn't room in the car."

Connington chuckled warmly and mellifluously. "I'll drive, and you can sit on Hawks' lap. Just like Charlie McCarthy."

Hawks pulled his glance away from Barker's face and said sharply, "I'll drive."

Connington chuckled again. "Sam Latourette didn't get the job with Hughes Aircraft. Waxted's wanting him didn't make any difference. He showed up helpless drunk for his hiring interview this morning. I'll drive." He turned toward the double plate-glass doors and began walking out. He looked back over his shoulder. "Come along, friends," he said.

4

Claire Pack stood watching them from the head of the steps up to the lawn. She was wearing a one-piece skirtless cotton swimsuit cut high at the tops of her thighs, and was resting her hands lightly on her hips. As Connington shut off the engine and the three of them got out of the car, she raised her eyebrows. The narrow strings that served as straps for the swimsuit were dangling in loops around her upper arms.

"Well, Doctor!" she said with low-voiced gravity and a pucker of her lips, "I'd been wondering when you'd drop by again."

Connington, coming around the other side of the car, smiled watchfully at her and said, "He had to bring Al home. Seems there was a little hitch in the proceedings today."

She glanced aside at Barker, who was raising the garage doors with abrupt, crashing movements of his arms and body, all his attention obviously on what he was doing. She ran her tongue over the edges of her teeth. "What kind?"

"Now, I wouldn't know as to that. Why don't you ask Hawks?" Connington took a fresh cigar out of his case. "I like that suit, Claire," he said. He trotted quickly up the steps, brushing by her. "It's a hot day. Think I'll go find a pair of trunks and take a dip myself. You and the boys have a nice chat meanwhile." He walked quickly up the path to the house, stopped, lit the cigar, glanced sideward over his cupped hands, and stepped out of sight inside.

Barker got into his car, started it, and clashed the gears as he moved it into the garage nose-first. The trapped thunder of the exhaust rumbled loudly and sputtered down into silence.

"I think he'll be all right," Hawks said.

Claire looked down at him. She focused her expression into an open-faced innocence. "Oh? You mean, he'll be back to normal?"

Barker brought the garage doors down and passed Hawks with his head bent, striding intently as he thrust the ignition keys into his pocket. His face jerked up toward Claire as he climbed the steps. "I'm going upstairs. I may sack out. Don't wake me." He half-turned and looked at Hawks. "I guess you're stuck here, unless you want to take another hike. Did you think of that, Doctor?"

"Did you? I'll stay until you're up. I'll want to talk to you."

"I wish you joy of it, Doctor," Barker said, and walked away, with Claire watching him. Then she looked back down at Hawks. Through all this, she had not moved her feet or hands.

Hawks said, "Something happened. I don't know how much it means."

"You worry about it, Ed," she said, her lower lip glistening. "In the meantime, you're the only one left standing down there."

Hawks sighed. "I'll come up."

Claire Pack grinned.

"Come over and sit by the pool with me," she said when he reached the top of the steps. She turned away before he could answer, and walked slowly in front of him, her right arm hanging at her side. Her hand trailed back, and reached up to touch his own. She slackened her pace so that they were walking side by side, and looked up at him. "You don't mind, do you?" she said gently.

Hawks looked down at their hands for a moment, and as he did, she put the backs of her fingers inside his palm. He said slowly, "No—no, I don't think I mind," and closed his hand around hers.

She smiled and said, "There, now," in an almost childishly soft voice.

They walked to the edge of the pool and stood looking down into the water.

"Did Connington take a long time getting over his drunk the other day?" Hawks asked.

She laughed brightly. "Come on, now—what you mean is, why do I still let him hang around after his ferocious threats? Answer: why not? What can he do, really?" Her sidelong glance came up from a graceful turn of her head and shoulders, so that her hair flashed in the sun and her eyes were half-veiled behind the glimmer of her lashes. "Or do you think I'm under his Svengali spell?" she asked with mock-horror that left her wide-eyed and with her lips in a scarlet, open pout.

Hawks kept his eyes steadily on hers. "No, hardly that."

Her eyebrows blinked up and down pleasurably, and her mouth parted in a low, whispered laugh. She swayed her upper body toward him, and put her other hand on his arm. "Should I take that as a tribute? Al tells me you're a hard man to get small talk out of."

Hawks put his right hand around his own left wrist and held it, his arm crossed awkwardly in front of his body. "What else has Al told you about his work?" he asked.

She looked down at his arm. She said gravely and confidentially, "You know, if I get too close to you, you can always dive into the pool." Then she grinned to herself again, keeping her face toward him to let him see it, and, taking her hands away, sank down to lie on one hip in the grass, her head bent so she could watch the surface of the water. "I'm sorry," she said without looking up. "I said that just to see if you'd jump. Connie's right about me, you know."

Hawks squatted angularly down next to her, watching the side of her turned-away face. "In what way?"

She put one hand down into the blue water and stirred it back and forth, silver bubbles trailing out between her spread fingers. "I can't know a man more than a few minutes without trying to get under his skin," she said in a pondering voice. "I have to do it. Measuring, I suppose you could call it." Her face flashed toward him. "And you can call that a Freudian pun if you want to." Then she had turned away again. A trail of splotched droplets on the pool's satiny concrete coaming began to shrink in the sun. Her voice was reflective and hidden again. "That's the way I am."

"Is it really? Or is saying so just another part of the process? You say everything for effect, don't you?"

Her face turned slowly, this time, and she looked at him with a faintly cynical undertone to her smile. "You're very quick, aren't you?" she pouted. "Are you sure I deserve all this concentration? After all, what good is it going to do you?" Her eyebrow arched, and she held that expression, her smile very slowly widening her lips.

"I don't decide what should interest me," Hawks said. "First something intrigues me. Then I study it."

"You must have curious instincts, mustn't you, then?" She waited for an answer. Hawks gave her none. She added, "In several senses of the word, I suppose." Hawks continued to look at her gravely, and she slowly lost the vivacity behind her expression. She rolled over suddenly on her back, her ankles crossed stiffly, and put her hands down flat on her thigh muscles. "I'm Al's woman," she said up at the sky.

"Which Al?" Hawks asked.

"What's happening to him?" she said, moving only her lips. "What are you doing to him?"

"I don't know, exactly," Hawks said. "I'm waiting to find out."

She sat up and twisted to face him, her breasts moving under the loose top. "Do you have any kind of a conscience?" she asked. "Is there anyone who isn't defenseless before you?"

He shook his head. "That kind of question doesn't apply. I do what I have to do. Only that."

She seemed to be almost hypnotized by him. She leaned closer.

"I want to see if Al's all right," Hawks said, getting up.

Claire arched her neck and stared up at him. "Hawks," she whispered.

"Excuse me, Claire." He stepped around her drawn-up legs and moved toward the house.

"Hawks," she said hoarsely. The top of the swimsuit was almost completely off the upper faces of her breasts. "You have to take me tonight."

He continued to walk away.

"Hawks—I'm warning you!"

Hawks flung open the house door and disappeared behind the sun-washed glass.

5

"How'd it go?" Connington laughed from the shadows of the bar at the other end of the living room. He came forward, dressed in a pair of printed trunks, his stomach cinched by the tight waistband. He was carrying a folded beach shirt over his arm and holding a pewter pitcher and two glasses. "It's a little like a silent movie, from here," he said, nodding toward the glass wall facing out onto the lawn and pool. "Hell for action, but short on dialogue."

Hawks turned and looked. Claire was still sitting up, staring intently at what must have been a barricade of flashing reflections of herself.

"Gets to a man, doesn't she?" Connington chuckled. "Forewarned is not forearmed, with her. She's an elemental—the rise of the tides, the coming of the seasons, an eclipse of the Sun." He looked down into the pitcher, where the ice at the top of the mixture had suddenly begun to tinkle. "Such creatures are not to be thought of as good or bad," he said through pinched lips. "Not by mortal men. They have their own laws, and there's no gainsaying them." His breath puffed into Hawks' face. "They are born among us—car hops, dice girls, Woolworth's clerks—but they rise to their heritage. Woe to us, Hawks. Woe to us who would pursue them on their cometary track."

"Where's Barker?"

Connington gestured with the pitcher. "Upstairs. Took a shower, threatened to disembowel me if I didn't get out of his way in the hall, went to bed. Set the alarm for eight o'clock. Put down a tumblerful of gin to help him. "Where's Barker?" Connington repeated. "Dreamland, Hawks— whatever dreamland it was that awaited him."

Hawks looked at his wrist watch.

"Three hours, Hawks," Connington said. "Three hours, and there is no Master in this house." He moved around Hawks to the outside door. "Yoicks!" he yapped twistedly, raising the pitcher in Claire's direction. He pushed clumsily at the door with his shoulder, leaving a damp smear on the glass. "Tally ho!"

Hawks moved farther into the room, toward the bar. He searched behind it, and found a bottle of Scotch. When he looked up from putting ice and water into a glass, he saw that Connington had reached Claire and was standing over her. She lay on her stomach, facing the pool, her chin resting on her crossed forearms. Connington held the pitcher, pouring awkwardly into the two glasses in his other hand.

Hawks walked slowly to the leather-covered settee facing the windows, and sat down. He put the edge of his glass to his lips, and rested his elbows on his thighs. He put both hands around his glass, holding it lightly, and tilted it until he could sip at it. The lower half of his face was washed by reddish sunlight mottled with faint amber dispersions and glassy points of shifting light. The arch of his nose and the upper part of his face were under a curtain of shadow.

Claire rolled half over and stretched up an arm to take the glass Connington handed down. She perfunctorily saluted Connington's glass and took a drink, her neck arching. Then she rolled back, resting her raised upper body on her elbows, her fingers curled around the glass she set down on the pool coaming. She continued to look out over the water.

Connington sat down on the edge of the pool beside her, dropping his legs into the water. Claire reached over and wiped her arm. Connington raised his glass again, held it up in a toast, and waited for Claire to take another drink. With a twist of her shoulders, she did, pressing the flat of her other hand against the top of her suit.

The sunlight slanted in from behind Connington and Claire Pack; their profiles were shadowed against the brilliant ocean and sky.

Connington refilled their glasses.

Claire sipped at hers. Connington touched her shoulder and bent his head toward her. Her mouth opened in laughter. She reached out and touched his waist. Her fingers pinched the roll of flesh around his stomach. Her shoulder rose and her elbow stiffened. Connington clutched her wrist, then moved up to her arm, pushing back. He twisted away, hurriedly set his glass down, and splashed into the pool. His hands shot out and took her arms, pulling them forward.

Light dashed itself into Hawks' face and filled his eye-

sockets as the sun's disk slid an edge down into sight under
the eaves of the roof. He dropped his lids until his eyes
were looking out through the narrow mask of his lashes.

Keeping his hold on Claire's wrists, Connington doubled
his bent-kneed legs forward, planted his feet against the side
of the pool, and strained himself out flat. Claire came sliding
into the water on top of him, and they weltered down out
of sight under the surface. A moment later, her head and
shoulders broke out a few feet away, and she stroked evenly
to the ladder, climbing out and stopping at the poolside to
pull the top of her suit back up over her breasts. She picked
her towel from the grass with one swoop of her arm, threw
it around her shoulders, and walked quickly off out of sight
to the left, toward the other wing of the house.

Connington stood in the pool, watching her. Then he
jumped forward, and thrashed up to the steps at the shallow
end, climbing out with water pouring down from his shoulders and back. He took a few strides in the same direction.
Then his face snapped toward the glass wall. He changed
direction obliquely, and, at the corner of the pool, did a flat
dive back into the water. He swam forward, toward the
diving board. For some time afterward, until the sun was
entirely in sight and the room where Hawks was sitting was
filled with red, the sound of the thrumming board came
vibrating into the timbers of the house at sporadic intervals.

At ten minutes to eight, a radio began to play loud jazz
upstairs. Ten minutes later, the electric blat of the radio's
alarm roiled the music, and a moment after that there was
a brittle crash, and then only the occasional sound of Barker
stumbling about and getting dressed.

Hawks went over to the bar, washed out his empty glass,

and put it back in its rack. He looked around. There was night outside the windows, and the only illumination came from the balcony at the end of the room, where the stairs led down from the second floor. Hawks reached out and turned on a standing lamp. His shadow flung itself against the wall.

6

Barker came down carrying a half-filled squareface bottle. He saw Hawks, grunted, hefted the bottle and said, "I hate the stuff. It tastes lousy, it makes me gag, it stinks, and it burns my mouth. But they keep putting it in your hands, and they keep saying 'Drink up!' to each other, and 'What's the matter, Charlie, falling a little behind, there? Freshen up that little drinkee for you?' Until you feel like a queer of some kind, and a bore for the times you say you don't want another one, positively. And they fill their folklore with it, until you wouldn't dream you were having a good time unless you'd swilled enough of the stuff to poison yourself all the next day. And they talk gentleman talk about it—ages and flavors and brands and blends, as if it wasn't all ethanol in one concentration or another. Have you ever heard two Martini drinkers in a bar, Hawks? Have you ever heard two shamans swapping magic?" He dropped into an easy chair and laughed. "Neither have I. I synthesize my heritage. I look at two drunks in a saloon, and I extrapolate toward dignity. I suppose that's sacrilege."

He put a cigarette into his mouth, lit the end, and said

through the smoke, "But it's the best I can do, Hawks. My father's dead, and I once thought there was something good in shucking off my other kin. I wish I could remember what that was. I have a place in me that needs the pain."

Hawks went back to the settee and sat down. He put his hands on his knees and watched Barker.

"And talk," Barker said. "You're not fit company for them if you don't say "Eyther" and "nyther" and "tomahto." If you've got a Dad, you're out. They only permit gentlemen with fathers into their society. And, yeah, I know they licked me on that. I wanted to belong—oh, God, Hawks, how much I wanted to belong—and I learned all the passwords. What did it get me? Claire's right, you know—what did it get me? Don't look at me like that. I know what Claire is. You know I know it. I told you the first minute I met you. But did you ever stop to think it's all worth it to me? Every time she makes a pass at another man, I know she's comparing. She's out on the open market, shopping. And being shopped for. I don't have any collar around her neck. She's not tame. I'm not a habit to her. I'm not something she's tied to by any law. And every time she winds up coming back to me, you know what that proves? It proves I'm still the toughest man in the pack. Because she wouldn't stay if I wasn't. Don't kid yourself—I don't know what you think about you and her, but don't kid yourself."

Hawks looked at Barker curiously, but Barker was no longer watching him.

"If she could see me, Hawks—if she could *see* me in that place!" Barker's face was aglow. "She wouldn't be playing footsie with you and Connington tonight—no, not if she could see what I do up there.... How I dodge, and

duck, and twist, and inch, and spring, and wait for the—
the—"

"Easy, Barker!"

"Yeah. Easy. Slack off. Back away. It bites." Barker
coughed out bitterly, "What're you doing here, anyway,
Hawks? Why aren't you marching down that road again
with your ass stiff and your nose in the air? You think it's
going to do you any good, you sitting around here? What're
you waiting for? For me to tell you sure, a little sleep and
a little gin and I'm fine, just fine, Doctor, and what time
do you want me back tomorrow? Or do you want me to
crack wide open, so you can really move in on Claire?
What've you been doing while I was asleep? Playing sticky-
fingers with her? Or did Connington weasel you out of the
chance?" He looked around. "I guess he must have."

"I've been thinking," Hawks said.

"What about?"

"What you wanted me here for. Why you came straight
to me and asked me to come. I was wondering whether you
hoped I could make you go back again."

Barker raised the bottle to his mouth and peered at Hawks
over it as he drank. When he lowered it, he said, "What's
it like, being you? Everything that happens has to be twisted
around to suit you. Nothing is ever the way it looks, to
you."

"That's true of everyone. No one sees the world that
others see. What do you want me to do: be made of brass?
Hollow, and more enduring than flesh? Is that what you
want a man to be?" Hawks leaned forward, tight creases
slashing down across his hollow cheeks. "Something that
will still be the same when all the stars have burned out and

the universe has gone cold? That will still be here when everything that ever lived is dead? Is that your idea of a respectable man?"

"A man should fight, Hawks," Barker said, his eyes distant. "A man should show he is never afraid to die. He should go into the midst of his enemies, singing his death song, and he should kill or be killed; he must never be afraid to die; he must never be afraid to meet the tests of his manhood. A man who turns his back—who lurks at the edge of the battle, and pushes others in to face his enemies—" Barker looked suddenly and obviously at Hawks. "That's not a man. That's some kind of crawling, wriggling thing."

Hawks got up, flexing his hands uncertainly, his arms awkward, his face lost in the shadows above the lamp's level. His calves pressed back against the leather of the settee, thudding it lightly against the wall. "Is that what you wanted me here for? So no one could say you wouldn't clasp the snake to your bosom?" He bent his head forward, peering down at Barker. "Is that it, warrior?" he asked inquisitively. "One more initiation rite? You've never been afraid to take your enemies in and give them shelter, have you? A truly brave man wouldn't hesitate to lodge assassins in his house, and offer them food and drink, would he? Let Connington the back-stabber come into your house. Let Hawks the murderer do his worst. Let Claire egg you on from one suicidal thing to the next, ripping off a leg here, a piece of flesh another time. What do you care? You're Barker, the Mimbreño warrior. Is that it?—But now you won't fight. Suddenly, you don't want to go back into the formation. Death was too impersonal for you. It didn't care how brave you were, or what preparatory rites you'd passed

through. That was what you said, wasn't it? You were out-
raged, Barker. You still are. What is Death, to think nothing
of a full-fledged Mimbreño warrior?

"*Are* you a warrior?" he demanded. "Explain that part
of it to me. What have you ever done to any of us? When
have you ever lifted a finger to defend yourself? You see
what we're about, but you do nothing. You're afraid to be
thought a man who wouldn't fight, but what do you fight?
The only thing you've ever done to me is threatened to pick
up your marbles and go home. No—sports cars and ski-
slopes, boats and airplanes: that's the kind of thing you
strive against. Things and places where you control the
situation—where you can say, as you die, that you know
the quality of the man you have killed. Things and places
where the fatal move can always be traced to the carelessness
or miscalculation of Barker, the killer, who has finally succeeded in overcoming his peer, Barker the warrior. Even in
the war, did you fight hand-to-hand, on open ground? You
were only an assassin like the rest of us, striking from the
dark, and if you were caught, it was your own fault. What
worthy enemy, besides yourself, have you ever met?

"I think you are afraid, Barker—afraid that no one else
who killed you would understand what a warrior you are.
How can you trust strangers to know you for what you
are? But a warrior is never afraid. Even within himself.
Is that what explains it, do you think, Barker? Is that the
trap you're caught in? In the far reaches of your mind,
do you suppose it's all been reasoned out, and kept safe—
that you must live among your enemies, to prove your
bravery, but dare not meet them in combat for fear of
dying unknown? Do you suppose that's why a stranger

has only to threaten you in order to become drawn into your life? And why you will let him nibble and rasp you to death, slowly, but will never turn and face him, and acknowledge that you are in a fight for your life? Because if you only let yourself be whittled at, the process may take years, and anything might happen to interrupt it, but if you fight, then it will be over immediately, and you might have lost, and died unsung?" Hawks looked quizzically at Barker. "I wonder," he said in a bemused voice, "I wonder whether that might not explain it."

Barker came quietly upward out of his chair. "Who are you to tell me these things, Hawks?" he said, calmly studying him. He reached behind his back without moving his eyes and set the bottle down on the small table beside the chair.

Hawks rubbed his palms over the cloth of his jacket. "Think about what happened to you today. You had thought the formation was something like an elaborate ski-slope, hadn't you, Barker? Just another dangerous, inexorable place, like many places men have been before.

"But there were no rules to explain what had killed you, when you died. You had gone beyond the charts. You couldn't say to yourself, as you died, that you had misinterpreted the rules, or failed to obey them, or tried to overcome them. There were no rules. No one had found them out. You died ignorant of what killed you. And there had been no crowd to applaud your skill or mourn your fate. A giant hand reached down and plucked you from the board—for what reason, no one knows. Suddenly, you knew that where you were was not a ski-slope at all, and all your skills were nothing. You saw, as clearly as anyone could ever see it, the undisguised face of the unknown universe. Men have put masks on it, Barker, and disarmed parts of it, and thought to themselves that they knew all of it. But they only know the parts they know. A man hurtling down a ski-slope has not learned the workings of gravity and friction. He has only learned how to deal with them in that particular situation, for all that he soars above them and lands safely. For all that the crowd sighs to watch a man overcome things that once killed men without mercy. All your jumping skills will not help you if you fall from an airplane without a parachute. All your past soaring and safe landing will not temper gravity then. The universe has resources of death which we have barely begun to pick at. And you found that out.

"Death is in the nature of the universe, Barker. Death is only the operation of a mechanism. All the universe has been running down from the moment of its creation. Did you expect a *machine* to care what it acted upon? Death is like sunlight or a falling star; they don't care where they fall. Death cannot see the pennants on a lance, or the wreath of glory in a dying man's hand. Flags and flowers are the inventions of life. When a man dies, he falls into enemy hands—an ignorant enemy, who doesn't merely spit on banners but who doesn't even know what banners are. No ordinary man could stand to find that out. You found it out today. You sat in the laboratory and were speechless at the injustice of it. You'd never thought that justice was only another human invention. And yet a few hours' sleep and a little gin *have* helped you. The shock has worn down. All human shocks wear off—except the critical one. You're not helpless now, like Rogan and the others are. Somehow, the creation inside your brain still lurches on. Why is that? How is it that dying didn't topple your foundations, if they are what you thought they were?

"Do you know why you're still sane, Barker? I think I do. I think it's because you have Claire, and Connington, and myself. I think it was because you had us to run to. It isn't really Death that tests your worth for you; it's the menace of dying. Not Death, but murderers. So long as you have us about you, your vital parts are safe."

Barker was moving toward him, his hands half-raised.

Hawks said, "It's no use, Barker. You can't do anything to me. If you were to kill me, you would have proved you were afraid to deal with me."

"That's not true," Barker said, high-voiced. "A warrior kills his enemies."

Hawks watched Barker's eyes. "You're not a warrior, Al," he said regretfully. "Not the kind of warrior you think you want to be. You're a man, that's all. You want to be a worthy man—a man who satisfies his own standards, a man whose stature is his own. That's all. That's enough."

Barker's arms began to tremble. His head tilted to one side, and he looked at Hawks crookedly, his eyes blinking. "You're so smart!" he panted. "You know so damned much! You know more about me than I do. How is that, Hawks— who touched your brow with a golden wand?"

"I'm a man, too, Al."

"Yes?" Barker's arms sank down to his sides. "Yes? Well, I don't like you any better for it. Get out of here, man, while you still can." He whirled and crossed the room with short, quick, jerking steps. He flung open the door. "Leave me to my old, familiar assassins!"

Hawks looked at him and said nothing. His expression was troubled. Then he set himself into motion and walked forward. He stopped in the doorway and stood face to face with Barker.

"I have to have you," he said. "I need your report in the morning, and I need you to send up there into that thing, again."

"Get out, Hawks," Barker answered.

"I told you," Hawks said, and stepped out into the darkness.

Barker slapped the door shut. He turned away toward the corridor leading into the other wing of the house, his neck taut and his mouth opening in a shout. It came almost inaudibly through the glass between himself and Hawks: "Claire? Claire!"

7

Hawks walked out across the rectangle of light lying upon the lawn, until he came to the ragged edge that was the brink of the cliff above the sea. He stood looking out over the unseen surf, with the loom of sea mist filling the night before him.

"An dark," he said aloud. "An dark and nowhere starlights." Then he began walking, head down, along the edge of the cliff, his hands in his pockets.

When he came to the flagstoned patio between the swimming pool and the far wing of the house, he passed by the metal table and chairs in its center, picking his way in the indistinct light.

"Well, Ed," Claire said sadly from her chair on the other side of the table. "Come to join me?"

He turned his head in surprise, then sat down. "I suppose."

Claire had changed into a dress, and was drinking a cup of coffee. "Want some of this?" she offered in a soft, uncertain voice. "It's a chilly evening."

"Thank you." He took the cup as she reached it out to him, and drank from the side away from the thick smear of lipstick. "I didn't know you'd be out here."

She chuckled ironically. "I get tired of opening doors and finding Connie on the other side. I've been waiting for Al to wake up."

"He's up."

"I know."

He passed the coffee cup back to her. "Did you hear it all?"

"I was in the kitchen. It—it was quite an experience, hearing myself talked about like that." She put the coffee down with a chatter of the cup against the saucer, and hugged herself, her shoulders bent, while she stared down toward the ground.

Hawks said nothing. It was almost too dark to see facial expressions across the table's diameter, and he closed his eyes for a moment, holding them tightly shut, before he opened them again and turned sideways in his chair, one hand resting on the table with its fingers arched as he leaned toward her.

"I don't know why I do it, Hawks," she said. "I don't know. But I *do* treat him as if I hated him. I do it to everybody. I can't meet anybody without turning into a bitch."

"Women, too?"

She turned her face toward him. "What woman would stay around me long enough for me to really get started? And what man is going to ignore the female part of me? But I'm a human being, too; I'm not just something that— that's all physical. But nobody *likes* me, Hawks—nobody ever shows any interest in the human *being* part of me!"

"Well, Claire . . ."

"It doesn't feel good, Hawks, hearing yourself talked about like that. 'I know what she is—by God, I know what she is.' *How* does he know? When has he ever tried to *know* me? What's he ever done to find out what I think, what I feel? And Connington—trying to maneuver me, trying to work things around so I'll give in to him. Getting Al involved in something he's sure will foul him up so badly I won't want him any longer. What gives him the idea it's got to be Connington for me if I go away from Al? Just because Connie's around all the time—because he doesn't have sense enough to go away after he's been licked? Is it my fault he hangs around? He doesn't get anything for it. All it does is get Al angry once in a while."

"Doesn't that make him useful to you?" Hawks asked.

"And you—" Claire burst out. "So damned sure nothing can touch you without permission! Making smart cracks. 'Egging' Al on is what I'm supposed to be doing! Well, listen, could I make a brick fly? Could I turn an ostrich into a swan? If he wasn't the way he was, what could I do to him? I don't tell him to go out and do these things. And I tried to keep him away from you—after you left, that first day, I tried to get him to quit! But all he did was get jealous. And that wasn't what I was trying to do! I've never made a pass at you before today—not a real pass—I was just, I don't know, just doing business as usual, you could say—and you know that!"

She reached across the table with a swift gesture and took his hand. "Do you have any idea of how lonely I get? How much I wish I wasn't me at all?" She pulled blindly at his hand. "But what can I do about it? How am I going to change anything now?"

"I don't know, Claire," Hawks said. "It's very hard for people to change themselves."

"But I don't *want* to hate myself, Hawks! Not all my life, like this! What do all of you think I am—blind, deaf, stupid? I know how decent people act—I know what bitchiness is, and what not being bitchy is. I was a child, once—I went to school, I was taught ethics, and morals, and understanding. I'm not something from *Mars*—do you all think I'm this way because I don't know any better?"

Hawks said haltingly, "All of us know better, I think. And yet each of us forgets, now and then. Some of us sometimes think we have to, for the sake of something we think needs it." His face was a mixture of expressions. "If that doesn't seem to make sense, I'm sorry. I don't know what else to tell you, Claire."

She jumped to her feet, still holding his hand, and came around to stand in front of him, bent forward, clasping his fingers in both hands. "You could tell me you like

me, Ed," she whispered. "You're the only one of them
who could look past my outsides and *like* me!"

He stood up as she pulled at his hand. "Claire—" he
began.

"No, no, no, Ed!" she said, putting her arms around him.
"I don't want to talk. I want to just *be*. I want someone to
just hold me and not think about me being a woman. I just
want to feel warm, for once in my life—just have another
human being near me!" Her arms went up behind his back,
and her hands cupped his neck and the back of his head.
"Please, Ed," she murmured, her face so close that her eyes
brimmed and glittered in the faraway light, and so that in
another moment her wet cheek touched his. "Give me that
if you can."

"I don't know, Claire . . ." he said uncertainly. "I'm not
sure you—"

She began kissing his cheeks and eyes, her nails combing
the back of his head. "Hawks," she choked, "Hawks, I'm
so lost. . . ."

His head bent, her fingers rigid behind it, the tendons
standing out in cords on the backs of her hands. Her lips
parted, and her leather sandals made a shuffling noise on
the patio stones. "Forget everything," she whispered as she
kissed his mouth. "Think only of me."

Then she broke away suddenly and stood a foot away
from him, the back of one hand against her upper lip,
her shoulders and hips lax. She was sighing rhythmically,
her eyes shining. "No—no, I can't hold out . . . not with
you. You're too much for me, Ed." Her shoulders rose
and she moved half a step toward him. "Forget about
liking me," she said from deep in her throat as she reached

toward him. "Just take me. I can always get someone else to like me."

Hawks did not move. She looked at him, arms outstretched, her face hungry. Then she lowered her arms slowly and cried out softly, "I don't blame you! I couldn't help it, but I don't blame you for what you're thinking. You think I'm some kind of nympho, who'll go wild for any man. You think because it's happening to me now, it always happens like this. You think that because you could do anything you wanted with me, then what I said about myself before wasn't true. You—"

"No," Hawks said. "But I don't think you believe it's true. You think it's something you can use because it sounds plausible. It does. It's true. And any time you grow afraid that a man may be about to find it out, you try to divert his attention with the only thing about you that you can imagine he'd be interested in. I think you're afraid of being in a world full of creatures called men. No matter how hard you say you try not to be that way, you always have to cut men down to your size." He took the handkerchief out of his breast pocket and wiped his mouth awkwardly. "I'm sorry," he said. "But that's the way it seems to me. Connington works on the premise that everyone has a weakness he can exploit. I don't know whether he's right or not, but yours is that you only give yourself to men you think will find your weakness. I wonder if you knew that?"

Her fingers dug at the dress fabric over her tensed thighs. "You're scared, Hawks," she said. "You're scared of a woman, just like so many of them are."

"Would you blame me? I'm frightened of many things. People who don't want to be people are among them."

"Why don't you just shut up, Hawks? What do you do, go through life making speeches? You know what you are, Hawks? You're a creep. A bore and a *creep*. A first-class bore. I don't want you around any more. I don't want to ever see you again."

"I'm sorry you don't want to be any different, Claire. Tell me something. You almost succeeded, a moment ago. You came very close. It would be foolish for me to deny it. If you had done what you tried to do with me, would I still be a creep? And what would you be, making up to a man you despise, for safety's sake?"

"Oh, get *out* of here, Hawks!"

"Does my being a creep make me incompetent to see things?"

"When are you going to stop trying? I don't want any of your *stinking* help!"

"I didn't think you did. I said so. That's really all I've said." He turned away toward the house. "I'm going to see if Al will let me use his phone. I need a ride away from here. I'm getting too old to walk."

"Got to *hell*, Hawks!" she cried out, following him at his own pace, a yard or two behind him.

Hawks walked away more quickly, his legs scissoring stiffly, his arms swinging through short arcs.

"Did you hear me? Get lost! Go on, get out of here!"

Hawks came to the kitchen door and opened it. Connington was sprawled back against a counter, his beach shirt and his swimming trunks spattered with blood and saliva from his mouth. Barker's left hand, tangled in his hair, was all that kept him from tipping over the high stool on which he was being held. Barker's right fist was drawn back, smeared and running from deep tooth-gashes over the bone of his knuckles.

"Just passed out, that's all," Connington was mumbling desperately. "Just passed out in her bed, that's all—she wasn't anywhere around."

Barker's forearm whipped out, and his fist slapped into Connington's face again. He said in a frantic voice, "This is just for wishing, Connie! I'm not going to stand for finding you in my woman's bed. That's all. I just can't let you get away with that!"

Connington fumbled apathetically behind him for a handhold. He made no effort to defend himself. "Only way you ever would. Find me there." He was crying without seeming to be aware of it. "I thought I had it figured out, at last. I thought today was the day. Never been able to make the grade with her. I can find the handle with everybody else. Everybody's got a weak spot. Everybody cracks, sometime, and lets me see it. Everybody. Nobody's perfect. That's the great secret. Everybody but her. She's got to slip sometime, but I've never seen it. Me, the hotshot personnel man."

"Leave him alone!" Claire screamed from behind Hawks. She clawed at Hawks' shoulder until he was out of the doorway, and then she raked at Barker, who jumped back with his hand clutching the furrows on his arm. "Get away from him!" she shouted into Barker's face, crouching with her feet apart and her quivering hands raised. She snatched

up a towel, wet a corner of it in the sink, and went to Connington, who was slumped back against the stool, staring at her through his watering eyes.

She bent against Connington and began frantically scrubbing his face. "There now, honey," she crooned. "There. There now." Connington put one hand up, palm out, his lax fingers spread, and she caught it, clutching it and pressing it to the base of her throat, while she rubbed feverishly at his smashed mouth. "I'll fix it, honey—don't worry. . . ."

Connington turned his head from side to side, his eyes looking blindly in her direction, whimpering as the cloth ground across the cuts.

"No, no, honey," she chided him. "No, hold still, honey! Don't worry. I need you, Connie. Please." She began wiping his chest, opening the top of the beach shirt and forcing it down over his arms, like a policeman performing a drunk arrest.

Barker said stiffly, "All right, Claire—that's it. I want your things out of here tomorrow." His mouth turned down in revulsion. "I never thought you'd turn carrion-eater."

Hawks turned his back and found a telephone on the wall. He dialed with clumsy haste. "This—this is Ed," he said, his throat constricted. "I wonder if you could possibly drive out to that corner on the highway, where the store is, and pick me up. Yes, I—I need a ride in, again. Thank you. Yes, I'll be there, waiting."

He hung up, and as he turned back, Barker said to him, his expression dazed, "How did you do it, Hawks?" He almost cried, "How did you manage this?"

"Will you be at the laboratory tomorrow?" Hawks said wearily.

Barker looked at him through his glittering black eyes. He flung out an arm toward Claire and Connington. "What would I have left, Hawks, if I lost you now?"

SIX

"You look tired," Elizabeth said as the studio's overhead fluorescents tittered into light and Hawks sat down on the couch.

He shook his head. "I haven't been working very hard. It's the same old story—when I was a boy on the farm, I'd wear myself out with physical labor, and I'd have no trouble getting to sleep. I'd wake up in the morning, and I'd feel wonderful; I'd be rested, and full of energy, and I'd know exactly what I had ahead of me that day, and I'd do it. Even when I was tired, I felt *right*; I felt as if what I'd done was proper. Even when I couldn't keep my eyes open after supper, my body was relaxed, and happy. I don't know if that's understandable if you haven't felt it, but that's how it was.

"But now I just sit around and think. I can't sleep at

night, and I wake up in the morning feeling worse than I did the day before. It takes me hours before I don't feel as if my body was cranky with me. I sometimes think it gets better during the day only because I go numb, not because the crankiness stops. I never feel right. I'm always full of aches and pains that come from nowhere. I look at myself in the mirror, and a sick man looks back at me—the kind of a man I wouldn't trust to do his share, if we were on a job together."

Elizabeth raised an eyebrow. "I think you could use some coffee."

He grimaced. "I'd rather have tea, if you have some."

"I think so. I'll see." She crossed the studio to the curtained-off corner where the hotplate and the cupboard were.

"Or—Look," he called after her, "I'm being silly. Coffee would be fine. If you don't have any tea."

They sat on the couch together, drinking tea. Elizabeth put her cup down on the table. "What happened tonight?" she asked.

Hawks shook his head. "I'm not entirely sure. Woman trouble, for one thing."

Elizabeth grunted. "Oh."

"Not the usual kind," Hawks said.

"I didn't think it would be."

"Why?"

"You're not the usual kind of man."

Hawks frowned. "I suppose not. At least, I don't seem to get the usual reactions from people. I don't know why."

"Do you want to know what it is with you and women?"

Hawks blinked at her. "Yes. Very much."

"You treat them like people."

"I do?" He shook his head again. "I don't think so. I've never been able to understand them very well. I don't know why they do most of the things they do. I've—As a matter of fact, I've had a lot of trouble with women."

Elizabeth touched his hand. "I wouldn't be a bit surprised. But that's beside the point. Now, you think about something: I'm a good deal younger than you are."

Hawks nodded, his expression troubled. "I've thought about that."

"Now you think about this, too: you're not charming, dashing, or debonair. You're funny-looking, as a matter of fact. You're too busy to spare much time for me, and even if you did take me out night-clubbing somewhere, you'd be so out of place that I couldn't enjoy it. But you do one thing: you let me feel that my rules are as worthwhile to me as yours are to you. When you ask me to do something, I know you won't be hurt if I refuse. And if I do it, you don't feel that you've scored a point in some kind of complex game. You don't try to use me, cozen me, or change me. I take up as much room in the world, the way you see it, as you do. Do you have any idea of how rare a thing that is?"

Hawks was puzzled. "I'm glad you feel that way," he said slowly, "but I don't think that's true. Look—" He got up and began pacing back and forth while Elizabeth sat watching, a faint smile on her face.

"Women—" he said earnestly, "women have always fascinated me. As a kid I did the usual amount of experimenting. It didn't take me long to find out life wasn't like what happened in those mimeographed stories we had circulating around the high school. No, there was something else—what, I don't know, but there was something about women. I don't mean the physical thing. I mean some special thing about women: some purpose that I couldn't grasp. What bothered me was that here were these other intelligent organisms, in the same world with men, and there had to be a purpose for that intelligence. If all women were for was the continuance of the race, what did they need intelligence for? A simple set of instincts would have done just as well. And as matter of fact, the instincts are there, so what was the intelligence for? There were plenty of men to take care of making the physical environment comfortable. That wasn't what women were for. At least, it wasn't what they *had* to have intelligence for. . . . But I never found out. I've always wondered."

Elizabeth smiled. "You still don't see that we're saying the same things about you."

Hawks sighed and said, "Maybe we are. But that doesn't tell me what I want to know."

Elizabeth said softly, "Maybe you'll find out some day soon. Meanwhile, why haven't you tried to make love to me?"

Hawks stared at her. "For Heaven's sake, Elizabeth, I don't know you well enough!"

"That's exactly what I mean about you," Elizabeth said, the blush fading from her face. "Now, Doctor, would you like another cup of tea?"

Elizabeth had gone back to work at her drawing table, sitting with her heels hooked over the top rung of her stool, a curl of smoke rising from the ash tray held in place by two map pins on the edge of the board. Now and then a wisp would drift into her face and make her squint. She would curse softly and smile at Hawks, who was sitting on a low hassock beside the table, his hand cupping his jack-knifed knees.

"I was in love with a girl at college," he said. "A very attractive girl, from Chicago. She was intelligent; she was, most of all, tactful. And she had seen and done so many things I hadn't—plays, opera, concerts: all the things you can have, in a city. I envied her tremendously because of it, and I admired her very much. The thing is, I never tried to share any of these things with her. I had the idea, I think, that if I asked her to tell me about these things, I would be taking them away from her—getting something from her that she had earned and I had no business filching. But I thought to myself that as fine a person as that could judge whether I was anything worthwhile or not. At least, I imagine that's how I looked at it. At any rate, I tried to share everything with her. I talked her ear off, as a matter of fact."

Elizabeth put her pencil down and raised her head to watch him.

"There were times when we were very close, and other times when we weren't. I was always in despair of losing her. And one day, just before we graduated, she said to me, very tactfully, 'Ed, why don't you just relax and take me out someplace where we can get a drink or two? We could dance a little, and go for a drive, and we could just park somewhere and not talk at all.' And something came over me," Hawks said. "In the blink of an eye, I was out of love with her. And I never went near her again.

"Why, exactly? I don't know. Just because I thought I was so wonderful that not being listened to was unimaginable? Hardly. I knew I was full of drivel. I knew that very little of what I had to say was either original or interesting. And I never talked to anyone but her. I could barely bring myself to keep up social conversations with other people. But I *loved* her, Elizabeth, and she had told me she didn't want to listen any longer, and I stopped loving her. It was as if she'd turned into a cobra. I began to tremble uncontrollably. I got away from her as fast as I could and went to my room—and sat there shaking. It must have been an hour before it stopped.

"She tried to get in touch with me several times. And there were times when I almost went out looking for her again. But it never worked out. I was out of love. And I was frightened . . . Once, during the war, I was trapped in a lab fire and barely got out in time. For a few moments, I was convinced I was going to die. That's the only time I've ever felt that same fear . . . Oh, yes," he said, "I have trouble with women."

"Maybe you just have trouble with dying."

His expression grew infinitely distant. The set of his face and body changed. "Yes," he said, "I do."

He stood up finally, his hands in his pockets, having sat without saying anything for a long time. "It's late. I'd better go," he said.

Elizabeth looked up from her work. "You're still on this project of yours?"

He smiled crookedly. "I suppose so. I'm assuming all the people I need on it will show up for work tomorrow."

"Do some of them stay home Saturdays?"

"Oh? Is tomorrow Saturday?"

"I thought that was what you meant."

"No. No, I didn't think of it. And the day after that will be Sunday."

Elizabeth raised her eyebrows and said innocently, "It usually works out that way, yes."

"Cobey'll be very upset," Hawks was saying, lost in thought. "He'll have to pay the technicians bonus-time rates."

"Who's Cobey?"

"A man, Elizabeth. Another man I know."

She drove him home, to the stuccoed pastel apartment house, built in the mid-1920s, where he had his one-and-one-half-room efficiency flat.

"I've never seen where you lived, before," she said, setting the parking brake.

"No," he agreed. His face was drawn with fatigue. He sat with his chin on his chest, his knees against the dashboard. "It's—" He waved his hand vaguely at the looming, tile-roofed bulk, the walls vined by cracks which had been plastered over and repainted with brush-wide stripes of paint fresher than the original overall coat. "It's a place."

"Don't you ever miss the farm country? Open fields? Woods? A clear sky?"

"There weren't many open fields," he said. "It was mainly chicken farming, and everything was filled up with one-and two-story lines of coops." He looked out the window. "Coops." He looked back at her. "You know, chickens are highly subject to respiratory ailments. They sigh and wheeze and snore, all night, by the thousands—a sound that hangs over entire townships, like the moaning of a distant crowd, weeping and deprived. Chickens. I used to wonder if they knew what we were—why we made them run in pens, and eat at feeding troughs, and drink at spigots. Why we kept the rain off them, and broke our backs carrying wet mash to them. Why we went into their coops, every week, and scraped their droppings out from under their roosts, and tried to keep the coops as clean of disease-breeding areas as possible. I wondered if they knew, and if that was why they groaned in their sleep. But of course, chickens are abysmally stupid. Of all the living things in this world, only Man thinks like Man."

He opened the car door, half turned to step out, and then stopped. "You know—You know," he began again, "I *do* talk a lot, when we're together." He looked at her apologetically. "You must get awfully bored with it."

"I don't mind."

He shook his head. "I can't understand you." He smiled gently.

"Would you like to?"

He blinked. "Yes. Very much."

"Maybe I feel the same way about you?"

He blinked again. "Well," he said. "Well, I've been sort of assuming that all long, haven't I? I never thought of that. I never did." He shook his head. He said ruefully, "Only Man thinks like Man." He got out of the car, and stood beside it looking in at her. "You've been very good to me tonight, Elizabeth. Thank you."

"I want you to call me again as soon as you can."

He frowned suddenly. "Yes. As soon as I can," he said in a troubled voice. He closed the door and stood tapping his fingers on the sill of the opened window. "Yes," he said. He grimaced. "Time runs on," he objected under his breath. "I'll—I'll call," he said to her, and walked away toward the apartment house, his head down, his arms hanging at his sides, the large hands opening and closing out of rhythm with his steps, his path a little erratic, so that he had wandered from one side of the walk to the other before he reached the apartment-house door and began fumbling for his key.

Finally, he got the door open. He turned, looked back, and waved stiffly, as if not sure he had really finished their conversation. Then he let the arm fall, and pushed the door open.

SEVEN

Barker came into the laboratory the next day with his eyes red-rimmed. His hands shook as he got into his undersuits.

Hawks walked up to him. "I'm glad to see you here," he said awkwardly.

Barker looked up and said nothing.

Hawks said, "Are you sure you're all right? If you're not feeling well, we can cancel until tomorrow."

Barker said, "Just stop worrying about me."

Hawks put his hands in his pockets. "Well. Have you been to see the navigating specialists?"

Barker nodded.

"Were you able to give them a clear account of yesterday's results?"

"They acted happy. Why don't you wait until they get it digested and put the reports on your desk? What does it matter to you what I find up there? Just as long as I keep making distance, and don't crack. Isn't that right? You don't care what happens to me; all I'm doing is blazing a trail so your smart technicians won't trip over anything when they go up there to take it apart, right? So what's it to you, unless you lose me and have to go find a new boy, right? And how would you do that? How many people do you suppose Connington has plans for in the back of his head? Not plans that lead to this place, right? So why won't you just leave me alone?"

"Barker——" Hawks shook his head. "No, forget it. There's no use talking."

"I hope you can stick to that idea."

Hawks sighed. "All right. There's one thing; this is going to go on day after day, now, astronomical conditions permitting. It won't stop until you've come out the other side of the formation. Once we start, it'll be difficult to interrupt our momentum. But if there's ever a time when you'd like to take a break——get some rest, work on your cars; anything——if it's at all possible, we'll do it. We——"

Barker's lips curled back. "Hawks, I'm here to do something. I intend to do it. It's all I want to do. All right?"

Hawks nodded. "All right, Barker." He took his hands out of his pockets. "I hope it doesn't take too long to do."

Hawks walked down the corridor until he came to the navigating section. He knocked, and stepped in. The men of the specialist team looked up, then went back to huddling over the large-scale map of the formation which occupied the twelve-foot-square table in the center of the room. Only the Coast Guard officer in charge came over to Hawks as the others patiently made marks on the large plastic sheet with bits of red chalk on the ends of long wooden pointers. One of them was standing at a tape recorder, his head cocked as he listened to Barker's voice.

The voice was low and strangled. "I *told* you!" it was saying. "There's a sort of blue cloud . . . and something that seems to be moving inside it. Not like something alive."

"Yes, we have that," a team member's patient voice replied. "But how far from where you were standing on the white sand hill was it? How many steps?"

"It's hard to say. Six or seven."

"Uh-huh. Now, you say that was directly on your right, the way you were faced? All right, now, then what did you do?"

"I walked about six feet out onto this ledge, and turned left to follow it around that red spire. Then I—"

"Did you notice where the blue cloud was, in relation to you, as you made that turn?"

"I was looking back over my right shoulder at it."

"I see. Would you turn your head to that angle, now, so I can get a better idea? Thank you. About twelve degrees from dead right. And it was still six or seven steps away in straight-line distance?"

The team member stopped the tape, ran it back, and began playing it again. He made a note on a work sheet.

The Coast Guard officer asked Hawks, "Can I help you with anything, Doctor? We'll have all this written up and ready for you in a few hours. As soon as it's done, we'll shoot it right up to your office."

Hawks smiled. "I didn't come here to chivvy you along or get underfoot. Don't worry, Lieutenant. I just wanted to know how it looks in general. Is he making enough sense to be of any help to you?"

"Doing fine, sir. His descriptions of things in there don't agree with anything the other reports gave us—but then nobody seems to see the same things. What counts is that the hazards are always located in the same relative positions. So we know there's *something* there, and that's enough." The lieutenant, a lean, habitually gloomy man, smiled. "And this is a lot better than trying to make sense out of a few scribbles from a slate. He's given us a tremendous amount to work with, just in this one trip." The lieutenant rubbed the back of his neck. "It's kind of a relief. There was a while there when we were beginning to be pretty sure we'd be eligible for retirement before that thing"—he nodded toward the map—"got itself finished."

Hawks smiled without amusement. "Lieutenant, if I weren't able to make the phone call to Washington that I can make, this job would have been all finished right now."

"Oh. I guess we'd better take good care of him, then." The lieutenant shook his head. "I hope he lasts. He's a little on the hard-to-get-along-with-side, for us. But you can't have everything. I guess if you've finally got a man who works out smoothly on the science part of this, that's the main thing, even if it's not all peaches and cream down here on the practical end."

"Yes," Hawks said. The man at the tape recorder shut the machine off, walked to the map table, tightened a piece of chalk in the socket of his pointer and, reaching out, made a delicate scarlet fleck-mark on the white plastic. He looked at it critically and then nodded with satisfaction.

Hawks nodded, too. He said, "Thank you, Lieutenant," to the officer, and went up to his office.

That day, the elapsed time Barker was able to survive within the formation was raised to four minutes, thirty-eight seconds.

On the day that the elapsed time was brought to six minutes, twelve seconds, Connington came to see Hawks in his office.

Hawks looked up curiously from behind his desk. Connington walked slowly across the office. "Wanted to talk to you," he mumbled as he sat down. "It seemed as if I ought to." His eyes searched restlessly back and forth.

"Why?" Hawks asked.

"Well—I don't know, exactly. Except that it wouldn't feel right, just sort of letting it drop. There's—I don't know, exactly, what you'd call it, but there's a pattern to life. . . . Ought to be a pattern, anyhow: a beginning, a middle, and an end. Chapters, or something. I mean, there's got to be a pattern, or how could you control things?"

"I can see that it might be necessary to believe that," Hawks said patiently.

"You still don't give an inch, do you?" Connington said.

Hawks said nothing, and Connington waited a moment, then let the matter drop. "Anyhow," he said, "I wanted you to know I was leaving."

Hawk sat back in his chair and looked at him expressionlessly. "Where are you going?"

Connington gestured vaguely. "East. I'll find a job there, I guess."

"Is Claire going with you?"

Connington nodded, his eyes on the floor. "Yes, she is."
He looked up and smiled desperately. "It's a funny way to
have it end up, isn't it?"

"Exactly the way you planned it," Hawks pointed out.
"All but the part about eventually becoming company president."

Connington's expression set into a defiant grin. "Oh, I
didn't really figure it was as sure a thing as that. I just
wanted to see what happened when I put some salt on your
tail." He stood up quickly. "Well, I guess that's that. I just
wanted to let you know how it all came out in the end."

"Well, no," Hawks said. "Barker and I are still not finished."

"*I* am," Connington said defiantly. "I've got my part of
it. Whatever happens from now on doesn't have anything
to do with me."

"Then you're the winner of the contest."

"Sure," Connington said.

"And that's what it always is. A contest. And then a
winner emerges, and that's the end of that part of everyone's
life. All right. Goodbye, Connington."

"Goodbye, Hawks." He turned away, and hesitated. He
looked back over his shoulder. "I guess that was all I wanted
to say."

Hawks said nothing.

"I could have done it with a note or a phone call." At
the door, he said, "I didn't have to do it at all." He shook
his head, puzzled, and looked to Hawks as if for an answer
to a question he was asking himself.

Hawks said gently, "You just wanted to make sure I knew
who the winner was, Connington. That's all."

"I guess," Connington said unsurely, and walked slowly out.

The next day, when the elapsed time was up to six minutes, thirty-nine seconds, Hawks came into the laboratory and said to Barker, "I understand you're moving into the city, here."

"Who told you?"

"Winchell." Hawks looked carefully at Barker. "The new personnel director."

Barker grunted. "Connington's gone East, someplace." He looked up with a puzzled expression on his face. "He and Claire went out to get her stuff yesterday, while I was here. They smashed all those windows looking from the living room out on the lawn. I'll have to have them all replaced before I can put the place up for sale. I never thought he was like that."

"I wish you'd keep the house. I envy it."

"That's none of your business, Hawks."

But, nevertheless, the elapsed time had been brought up to six minutes, thirty-nine seconds.

On the day that the elapsed time was brought up to seven minutes, twelve seconds, Hawks was in his office, tracing his fingertip down the crumbled chart, when his desk telephone rang.

He glanced aside at it with a flicker of his eyes, hunched his shoulders, and continued with what he was doing. His fingertip moved along the uncertain blue line, twisting between the shaded black areas, each marked with its instruction and relative time bearing, each bordered by its drift of red X's, as if the chart represented a diagram of a prehistoric beach, where one stumbling organism had marked its labored trail up upon the littered sand between the long rows of drying kelp and other flotsam which now lay stranded under the lowering sky. He stared down raptly at the chart, his lips moving, then closed his eyes, frowned, repeated bearings and instructions, opened his eyes and leaned forward again.

The telephone rang once more, softly but without stopping. He tightened his hand into a momentary fist, then pushed the chart aside and took the handset off its cradle. "Yes, Vivian," he said.

He listened, and finally said, "All right. Call the gatehouse, please, and clear Dr. Latourette for a visitor's pass. I'll wait for him here." He put the telephone down and looked around at the bare walls of his office.

Sam Latourette knocked softly on the door and came in, his mouth quirked into a shy half-smile, his footsteps slow and diffident as he crossed the room.

He was wearing a rumpled suit and an open-throated white shirt without a tie. There were fresh razor nicks on the underside of his jaw and on his neck, as if he had shaved only a few minutes ago. His hair was carefully combed; still damp from the water he had used on it, it lay in thick furrows with his scalp visible between them, as though someone had found an old papier-mâché bust of him and from an impulse of old fondness, had refurbished it as well as was possible under the circumstances.

"Hello, Ed," he said gently, extending his hand as Hawks got up quickly. "It's been a while."

"Yes. Yes it has. Sit down, Sam—Here; here's the chair."

"I hoped you could spare the time to see me," Latourette said, sinking down. He looked up apologetically. "Things must be moving along pretty fast now."

"Yes," Hawks said, lowering himself into his own chair. "Yes, pretty much so."

Latourette looked down at the chart, which Hawks had folded and put down on the far end of the desk. "It looks like I was wrong about Barker."

"I don't know." Hawks moved a hand toward the chart then withdrew it and put his hands back in his lap. "He's making progress for us. I suppose that's what counts." He watched Latourette uncertainly, his eyes restless.

"You know," Latourette said with that same embarrassed twist of his features, "I didn't want that job with Hughes Aircraft. I thought I did. You know. A man—a man wants to keep working. Anyway, that's what he's supposed to want."

"Yes."

"But you know I don't get drunk. I mean, I—I just don't. Oh, at a party, maybe. I used to. But not—Well, not because I'm mad and want to break things. I was never like that."

"No."

Latourette laughed, swallowing the sound. "I guess I was just trying to tell myself I really was mad at you. You know—trying to make myself feel like some kind of tragic figure. No—no, I didn't want to go to work. That's all, I guess. What I really wanted was to just go and sit in the sun. I mean, my job here was finished, anyway—and you had to start breaking Ted Gersten in. Would have had to, sooner or later, anyhow."

Hawks put his hands on the edge of his desk. "Sam," he said steadily, "I don't know to this day whether I did the right thing or not." He said, "I panicked, Sam. I got scared, because Barker had gotten to me."

Latourette said quickly, "That doesn't mean you were wrong. Where would any of us be if we didn't play a sudden hunch? Now and then, you have to move fast. You look back later, and you see that if you hadn't, everything would have gotten to be too much to handle. The backs of our minds are smarter than we are, sometimes." He pulled a cigarette out of his shirt pocket without looking down, his fingers plucking uncertainly into his pocket while he stared fixedly into the air, as if what he were saying had been thought out ahead of time, in some rehearsal of what he and Hawks would say to each other, and as if his actual attention was on something he was not yet sure he was ready to say.

"I'll be going into a hospital tomorrow," he went on. "It's pretty much time for it. I mean, I could stay out a little while longer, but this way it's over with. And, you know, I could stand to go on morphine . . . or whatever it is. It's getting pretty itchy," he said off-handedly. "And anyhow, the government sent a man around the other day. Didn't outright tell me to do anything, but I think they'd be happier if I was someplace where it doesn't matter what I say in my sleep." He made a sophisticated grin. "You know. Big Brother."

Hawks sat watching him.

"Anyhow—" Latourette waved a hand, unconscious of the cigarette he had been holding poised halfway to his lips ever since he had finally gotten it out of his pocket. "I'll be out of circulation." He looked down, said, "Oh," and put the end of the cigarette in his mouth. Rapidly taking a pack of matches from his coat pocket and striking a light, he puffed vigorously, waved the match out and leaned forward to flip it into Hawks' wastebasket, his face turned to concentrate on his attempt to hit the target. "So I was wondering if you might not think it a good idea to run off a dupe of me from my file tape. That way you could have me—I mean, you could have the dupe—around in the lab, in case some help would be handy now and then. I mean, you're so close to the climax of things, it might be handy to have me . . ." His voice trailed away. He watched Hawks out of the corner of his eye, blushing.

Hawks got up quickly and began readjusting the settings on the air-conditioning unit buried in the window behind his desk. The mechanical linkages to the control knobs were stiff, and thumped into their new positions with a corresponding metallic rattle from the dampers.

"Sam, you know your latest file tape is six months old. If we made a dupe of you from it, the dupe wouldn't even know the procedure we're using on the Moon shots now. He'd think it was April."

"I—I know that, Ed," Latourette said softly. "I didn't say you should give him my old job back. But I knew I was going to be duped from tape sometime. I mean, I— the dupe—wouldn't be surprised at what had happened. I'd thought about what it would be like. The dupe would be a trained man, and he'd understand the situation. He'd readjust quickly."

"Would he readjust to working under Gersten?" Hawks turned around, his back pressed against the air conditioner.

"It's not a matter of his understanding or not understanding what had happened. It's more than that. Look at it from his point of view. As far as he'd be concerned, one minute he'd been going into the transmitter for a scan as second-in-charge of the whole shooting match, and the next moment he'd be coming out of the receiver not just with six months gone by in an instant, not just with Gersten in charge over him, but with half a dozen other men in positions more crucial than his. All right—so he'd be you, he'd realize what had happened, he'd know he was a dupe. But would he *feel* it? How would you have felt, in April, if you'd gone in for that scan, knowing it was just routine stuff, that all that was going to happen was that a tape would be filed away and you'd go back to the rest of the day's work. And then, when you came out, it wasn't that way at all—the whole world had changed, and a hundred things had been done in ways you knew nothing about, and suddenly you were just another engineer, and even your old acquaintances didn't know how to talk to you, and Gersten was embarrassed toward you, and a total stranger named Barker seemed to have some sort of special hostility reserved for you? Think about it, Sam. Because that's exactly how the dupe would feel. And the biggest thing he'd feel would be the unfairness of it all. Sam—what do you want to do to yourself?"

Latourette said slowly, looking down at the floor, "To say nothing of not being able to understand what's happened to Ed Hawks—except that somehow I'd make things harder for him, instead of easier." He looked up. "My God, Ed, what's happened to me? What am I doing to both of us? All I ever wanted to do was help you, and somehow it's come out like this. I never should have come here today, Ed. I shouldn't have done this last thing to you."

"Why not?" Hawks wanted to know. "Don't you have a moral right to work on something you put so much of yourself into? Doesn't a dying man have any rights? Even the right to live through six months of cancer all over again?" He looked at Latourette. "You've thought about this. You've spent a lot of time on it. If I could expect an answer from anyone, it would be you: why can't you get what's due you?"

Latourette looked at him in distress. "Ed, I shouldn't have come here."

"Why not? All you did was panic, Sam. You felt things closing in on you, and you had to make a move. A man has to do something—he can't just wait to sink out of sight."

"No, I shouldn't have come here."

"Why not? Why can't a man stand up and make a protest against the things that are sweeping over him? Why should a man be at the mercy of things that pay him no attention?"

Latourette got to his feet. "I've made it worse," he said desperately. "I've piled another thing on you. I didn't mean to. The only thing I can do is walk out of here right now. Please, Ed—try to get this out of your mind." He walked quickly to the door, and stared at Hawks for one moment of incomprehension. "All I wanted at first was what was best for you. And then when I came here today, I still thought I wanted what was best for you. But I wanted something for myself, besides, and that ruined it. Somehow, it's all ruined. How do people get into these things?" he asked blindly. "Where is it arranged?"

Hawks said bitterly, "Why can't a man get what he deserves?"

"Ed, this is the worst thing I've ever done to you."

"Perhaps it's what I deserve. Sam, I wish—"

"Goodbye, Ed," Latourette said, terrified, and walked out. Hawks sat down, his eyes closed, his hands making aimless, quick, twitching gestures over the surface of the chart.

Hawks walked across the laboratory floor toward the transmitter. Gersten stepped up to him unexpectedly and said, "I tried to get hold of you a little while ago. Your secretary said Sam Latourette was in your office, and was it anything that couldn't wait."

Hawks looked at him. Gersten's face was pale. His lips were trembling.

Hawks said uncertainly, "I'm sorry about that. Sometimes Vivian forgets the relative importance of things." He peered at Gersten. "Was she impolite to you?" he asked with a puzzled frown.

"She was perfectly proper. And it wasn't anything that couldn't wait, under the circumstances." Gersten started to turn away.

"Wait," Hawks said. "What's wrong?"

Gersten turned back. He began to speak, then changed his mind. He waited a moment, and asked quietly, "Am I still on the job?"

Hawks said, "Why shouldn't you be?" Then his frown disappeared. "What made you think I wanted Sam back?" he asked slowly. He searched Gersten's face. "I've always thought of you as a very confident man. You do a good job for me." He put his palm behind his neck and stood kneading the rigid muscles with his fingertips. "As a matter of fact, I'd had the feeling that giving you more responsibility was something I probably should have done earlier. I'm—I'm sorry I didn't have time to get to know you better, sooner." He brought his hand down awkwardly, and shrugged. "That's bound to happen now and again. It's always a shame when it happens to a good man. But I don't know what else to say to you."

Gersten bit his lip. "Do you mean all of that? I never know what's in your mind."

Hawks' eyebrows rose. His lips twitched. "That's a strange thing for you to say to me."

Gersten shook his head in annoyance. "I don't know what you mean by that, either. Hawks—" He brought his glance up. "This is the best job I ever had. It's the most important job I ever had. I'm almost five years younger than you are. Whether I know this trade as well as you do is something else again. But assuming I do, what chance do you think I have of being where you are now, five years from now?"

Hawks frowned. "Well, I don't know," he said thoughtfully. "That depends, of course. Five years ago, I was begining to fumble around the edges of this thing—" He nodded toward the equipment around them. "It happened to be something with possible military applications, so it got quite a boost. If it had been something else, it might not be as far along toward practicality. But that's no criterion. What people will buy isn't necessarily what's best . . . if anything's best." He shrugged. "I just don't know, Ted. If you've got some basically new idea you're working out in your spare time, the way I was when I was with RCA, you might go pretty near anywhere with it." He shrugged again. "That would be pretty much up to you."

Gersten frowned at him. "I don't know. I don't know. I'm sorry if I let myself get into a swivet over nothing, just now." He smiled a quick, uncertain apology that disappeared. "I imagine you've got other things to think about besides cranky engineers. "But—" He seemed to gather himself up. "When I enlisted in the Army during the war," he said bluntly, "I applied for Officer Candidate's School. I was interviewed by a temporary lieutenant who'd been a buck sergeant since the days when they were civilizing 'em with a Krag underneath the starry flag. He interviewed me, he filled in all the proper questionnaire spaces, and then he turned the form over, licked the end of his pencil again, and wrote down, "This candate seems to have language difficulties. This language difficulties would probly keep him from exercising proper command of troops." Then he turned the form around, so I could read the confidential appraisal he'd made. And that was that." Gersten watched Hawks' face very carefully. "What do you think of that?"

Hawks blinked. "What did the Army do with you, after that?"

"They sent me to electronics school at Fort Monmouth."

"So you're not sure you'd be here today, if it wasn't for that?"

Gersten frowned. "I suppose so," he said finally. "It's not the way I've looked at it."

"Well, I don't know about you, Ted, but I would have made a terrible career officer in the Navy. I don't suppose being in the Army would have improved matters." He grimaced suddenly. "And let me worry about Sam Latourette."

Then he looked apologetically at Gersten. "Maybe after we've gotten over the hump with this project, we can get to know each other better."

Gersten said nothing. He looked at Hawks as if he could not decide what expression to put on his face. Then he half shrugged and said, "What I wanted to speak to you about, earlier, was this business with the signal amplifier array. Now, it seems to me that if we—"

They walked away together, talking shop.

The day after the elapsed time was brought up to seven minutes, forty-nine seconds, the transmitter had to be shut down because the angle of shoot would have included too much of the Earth's ionosphere. The maintenance crews set to work on their periodic rebuilding schedule. Hawks worked with them.

On the day they were able to shoot again, Barker came into the laboratory at the proper time.

"You look thinner," Hawks said.

"You don't look so hot yourself."

On the day that the elapsed time was brought to eight minutes, thirty-one seconds, Benton Cobey called Hawks into his office for a conference.

Hawks came in, wearing a clean smock, looking carefully at the men around the conference table across the room from Cobey's desk. Cobey stood up from his chair at the head of the table.

"Dr. Hawks, you know Carl Reed, our Comptroller," he said, indicating the reserved, balding, raw-boned man who sat beside him, his ploughman's hands lying relaxed atop each other on the sheaf of bookkeeping work sheets he had brought with him.

"How do you do?" Hawks said.

"Well, thank you. And you?"

"And this is Commander Hodge, of course," Cobey said shortly, nodding toward the liaison naval officer who sat on his other side, his cap off and resting on the table, reflected in the glowing wood.

"Of course," Hawks said with a faint smile which Hodge answered in kind. He walked to the end of the table opposite Cobey and sat down. "What's the trouble?" he asked.

Cobey glanced aside at Reed. "We might as well get right to it," he said.

Reed nodded. He leaned slightly forward, his fingertips advancing the work sheets in Hawks' direction.

"These are the figures, here, on your laboratory equipment requisitions," he said.

Hawks nodded.

"Both for the original installation, and replacements over the past fiscal year."

Hawks nodded again. He looked toward Cobey, who was sitting with his hands tented, his elbows on the table and his thumbs under his chin, looking over his fingertips down at the work sheets. Hawks glanced aside at Hodge, who was running the side of his right index finger up and down one cheek, his ice-blue eyes apparently vacant, their corners crinkled into habitual crow's feet.

"Dr. Hawks," Reed said, "in looking over these, it first occurred to me that we ought to be looking for ways to manage this business more economically, if possible. And then it seems to me that we have done so."

Hawks looked at Reed.

Reed said, "Now, I've explained my idea to Mr. Cobey, and he agrees with me that it ought to be presented to you."

Cobey's mouth twitched.

"And so," Reed finished, "we checked with Commander Hodge on whether the Navy would be willing to consider a change in operating procedure, provided it didn't interfere with efficiency in any important way."

Hodge said, still without seeming to devote any great part of his attention, "We don't mind saving money. Especially when we're not free to have the appropriation itemized at congressional hearings."

Hawks nodded.

No one said anything, and then Cobey broke out, "Well, are you willing to listen, Hawks?"

Hawks said, "Of course." He looked around. "I'm sorry— I had no idea we were all waiting for me." He looked at Reed. "Go ahead, please."

"Well," Reed said, looking down at his figures, "it occurs to me that a lot of this equipment is just more of the same. I mean by that, here's an item for one hundred voltage dividers of a single type. And here's another one for—"

"Yes. Well, a good deal of our equipment consists of one particular component or another, linked into a series of similar components." Hawks' head was cocked to one side, and his eyes were watchful. "We have to handle a great many basically similar operations simultaneously. There was no time to design components with the capacity to carry out these functions. We had to use existing electronic designs and make up for their comparatively low capacity by using a great many of them." He paused for a moment. "It takes a thousand ants to carry away a cupful of sugar," he said at last.

"That's very apt, Hawks," Cobey said.

"I was trying to explain—"

"Go ahead, Reed."

"Well—" Reed leaned forward earnestly. "I don't want you to think I'm some kind of ogre, Dr. Hawks. But, let's face it, there's a lot of money tied up in that equipment, and as far as I can see, there's no reason why, if we've got a duplicating machine in the first place, we can't just"—he shrugged—"run off as many copies as we need. I can't see why they have to be built in our manufacturing division, or purchased from outside suppliers. Now, we've got a situation here where I can't even calculate a fixed operating cost. And—"

"Mr. Reed," Hawks said.

Reed stopped. "Yes?"

Hawks rubbed his face. "I appreciate your position. And I can see that what you've just proposed is completely reasonable, from that point of view. However—"

"All right, Hawks," Cobey said drily. "Get to the 'however.'"

"Well," Hawks said to Reed, "do you know the principles on which the scanner works—the duplicator?"

"Pretty roughly, I'm afraid," Reed said patiently.

"Well, pretty roughly, the duplicator takes a piece of matter and reduces it to a systematic series of electron flows. Electricity. A signal, like the signal that comes out of a radio sending set. Now, that signal is fed into these components—the same way, you might say, that it came in from the antenna of a radio receiver and was passed into the circuit inside it. When it comes out of the other end of the circuit, it doesn't go into a loudspeaker but is retransmitted to the Moon, having meanwhile been cross-checked for its accuracy. Now that's essentially what these components do— they inspect the signal for consistency. Now, the point is that the accuracy with which the original piece of matter is reconstructed—duplicated—depends on the consistency of the electron flows which arrive at the receiver. Therefore, if we were to use duplicated components to check the consistency of the signal with which we duplicate highly complicated objects, such as a living human being, we would be introducing an additional possibility for error which, in the case of a human being, works out higher than we can safely permit. Do you follow that?"

Reed frowned.

Cobey quirked his mouth up at one corner, looking down the table at Hawks.

Hodge picked up his cap and began adjusting the wire stiffening inside its white cover.

Finally, Reed said, "Is that all, Dr. Hawks?"

Hawks nodded.

Reed shrugged in embarrassment. "Well, look," he said, "I'm afraid I still don't see it. I can see that maybe your original equipment couldn't be duplicated, because your scanner wouldn't work without it, but—"

"Oh, it would *work* without it," Hawks interjected. "As I said, it's a control circuit. It's not primary."

Reed put his hands down sharply and looked at Cobey. He shook his head.

Cobey took a deep breath and let it out bitterly. "What do you say, Commander?"

Hodge put his cap down. "I think what Dr. Hawks means is that if you have an automatic lathe making automatic lathes, and you use these automatic lathes you've made to make more lathes, all it takes is for one part in any one of these lathes to slip, and pretty soon you've got a zillion lathes that're just so much junk."

"Well, God damn it, Hawks, why couldn't you put it that way?" Cobey demanded.

The day the elapsed time reached nine minutes, thirty seconds, Hawks said to Barker, "I'm worried. If your elapsed time grows much longer, the contact between M and L will become too fragile. The navigating team tells me your reports are growing measurably less coherent."

"Let 'em try going up there, then. See how much sense they can make out of it." Barker licked his lips. His eyes were hollow.

"That's not the point."

"I know what the point is. There's another point. You can stop worrying. I'm almost out the other side."

"They didn't tell me that," Hawks said sharply.

"They don't know. But I've got a feeling."

"A feeling."

"Doctor, all that chart shows is what I tell after I've done a day's work. It has no beginning and no end, except when I put the end to it." He looked around the laboratory, his face bitter. "All this plumbing, Doctor, and in the end it comes down to all revolving around one man." He looked at Hawks. "One man and what's in his mind. Or maybe two of us. I don't know. What's in your mind, Hawks?"

Hawks looked at Barker. "I don't pry into your mind, Barker. Don't set foot in mine. I have a telephone call to make."

He walked away across the laboratory, and dialed an outside number. He waited for the answer, and as he waited, he stared without focusing at the old, familiar blank wall. Suddenly he moved into a spasm of action and smashed the flat of his free hand violently against it. Then the buzz in the earpiece stopped with a click, and he said eagerly, "Hello? Elizabeth? This—this is Ed. Listen—Elizabeth—Oh, I'm all right. Busy. Listen—are you free tonight? It's just that I've never taken you to dinner or dancing, or anything. . . . Will you? I—" He smiled at the wall. "Thank you." He hung up the telephone and walked away. He looked back over his shoulder, and saw that Barker had been watching him, and he started self-consciously.

EIGHT

"Elizabeth—" he began, and then waved his arm in annoyance. "No. It was all going to come out in a rush. It does, so often."

They were standing atop an arm of rock that thrust out seaward into the surf. Hawks' collar was turned up, and he held his jacket together with one hand. Elizabeth was wearing a coat, her hands in its pockets, a kerchief over her hair. The Moon, setting on the horizon, reflected its light upon the traceries of clouds overhead. Elizabeth smiled up at him, her wide mouth stretching. "This is a very romantic spot you've brought us to, Edward."

"I—I was just driving. I didn't have any particular place in mind." He looked around. "I'm not full of cunning, Elizabeth—I'm full of logic, and reasoning, and God knows what else." He smiled self-consciously. "Though I suspect the worst—but that almost always comes afterward. I say to myself, 'Now, what am I doing here?' and then I have to know the answer. No, I have things—" He clutched at the air. "Things I want to say. Tonight. No later." He took a step forward, turned, and stood facing her, staring rigidly over her shoulder at the empty beach, the rise of the highway with his car parked on its shoulder, and the eastern sky beyond. "I don't know what shape they'll take. But they have to come out. If you'll listen."

"Please."

He shook his head at her, then forced his hands into his hip pockets and kept his body rigid.

"You know—You know, during the war, the Germans refused to believe microwave radar was practical. Their submarines were equipped with radar search receivers, to detect anti-submarine radar in use. But they only received comparatively long wave lengths. When we put microwave radar on our patrol planes and convoy escorts, we began picking them off at night, when they surfaced to charge their batteries. But, before that, in the early part of the war, we had to get hold of one of their receivers, so we could determine their limitations. As it happened, I was given one to work on. A destroyer's boarding party had managed to recover one from a submarine that had been depth-charged and forced to the surface, and then shelled. Our people ripped the set out just before the submarine sank. The receiver was sent on to the laboratory where I was, by special courier plane from an escort carrier, and then by car. I had it within twelve hours.

"Well, I put it down on my workbench and looked at it. The case was torn up by shrapnel, waterlogged . . . and terribly stained. There was smoke, there was oil, salt water corrosion, chemical fume contamination from the shellbursts—you know. And there were other kinds of debris on it. But I was a bright young man in those days, with a few commendations and my Reserve commission, and full of being a boy wonder—" Hawks grimaced. "I looked at the case, and in my mind, I said something spritely to myself on the order of, 'Hmm, shouldn't be too much trouble unraveling this. Just get some of this mess off the surface and—' And so forth. And all that time, the diluted blood I could see dried out in a smudge around the largest hole was just another part of the 'mess.' Some seaman, I thought to myself, very professionally, never having been to sea, some seaman was standing near it when the shells hit the conning tower. But when I prized the sheet-metal casing away, Elizabeth, there was a human *heart* in there, Elizabeth—in among the tubes and the wires."

After a while, Elizabeth said, "What did you do?"

"Well, after a while I came back and studied the receiver, and built a replica. And after that we used microwave radar and won the war.

"Listen—the thing is, people say when a man dies, 'Well, he had a full life, and when his time came, he went peacefully.' Or they say, 'Poor boy—he'd barely begun to live.' But the thing is, dying isn't an incident. It isn't something that happens to a man on one particular day of his life, soon or late. It happens to the *whole* man—to the boy he was, to the young man he was—to his joys, to his sorrows, to the times he laughed aloud, to the times he smiled. Whether it's soon or late, how can the dying man possibly feel it was *enough* of a life he lived, or not enough? Who measures it? Who can decide, as he dies, that it was *time?* Only the body reaches a point where it can't move any more. The mind—even the senile mind, fogged by the strangling cells of its body's brain—rational or irrational, broad or narrow; that never stops; no matter what, as long as one trickle of electricity can seep from one cell to another, still it functions; still it moves. How can any mind, ever, say to itself, 'Well, this life has reached its logical end,' and shut itself down? Who can say, 'I've seen enough'? Even the suicide has to *blow* his brains out, because he has to destroy the physical thing to evade whatever it is in his mind that will not let him rest. The mind, Elizabeth—intelligence; the ability to look at the universe; to care where the foot falls, what the hand touches—how can it help but go on, and on, drinking in what it perceives around it?"

His arm swept out in a long, stiff arc that swept over the beach and the sea. "*Look* at this! All your life, you'll have this, now! And so will I. In our last moments, we will still be able to look back, to *be* here again. Years away from here, and thousands of miles away from here, we would still have it. Time, space, entropy—no attribute of the universe can take this from us, except by killing us, by crushing us out.

"The thing is, the universe is *dying!* The stars are burning their substance. The planets are moving more slowly on their axes. They're falling inward toward their suns. The atomic particles that make it all up are slowing in their orbits. Bit by bit, over the countless billions of years, it's slowly happening. It's all running down. Some day, it'll stop. Only one thing in the entire universe grows fuller, and richer, and *forces* its way uphill. Intelligence—human lives—we're the only things there are that don't obey the universal law. The universe kills our bodies; it drags them down with gravity; it drags, and drags, until our hearts grow tired with pumping our blood against its pull, until the walls of our cells break down with the weight of themselves, until our tissues sag, and our bones grow weak and bent. Our lungs tire of pulling air in and pushing it out. Our veins and capillaries break with the strain. Bit by bit, from the day we're conceived, the universe rasps and plucks at our bodies until they can't repair themselves any longer. And in that way, in the end, it kills our brains.

"But our *minds* . . . There's the precious thing; there's the phenomenon that has nothing to do with time and space except to use them—to describe to itself the lives our bodies live in the physical Universe.

"Once my father took me out for a walk, late one night after a snowfall. We walked along, down a road that had just been ploughed. The stars were out, and so was the Moon. It was a cold, clear night, with the snow drifted and mounded, sparkling in the light. And on the corner where our road met the highway, there was a street lamp on a high pole. And I made a discovery. It was cold enough to make my eyes water, and I found out that if I kept them almost closed, the moisture diffused the lights, so that everything—the Moon, the stars, the street lamp—seemed to have halos and points of scattered light around it. The snow-banks seemed to glitter like a sea of spun sugar, and all the stars were woven together by a lace of incandescence, so that I was walking through a universe so wild, so wonderful, that my heart nearly broke with its beauty.

"For years, I carried that time and place in my mind. It's

still there. But the things is, the universe didn't make it. *I*
did. I saw it, but I saw it because I made myself see it. I
took the stars, which are distant suns, and the night, which
is the Earth's shadow, and the snow, which is water undergo-
ing a state-change, and I took the tears in my eyes, and I
made a wonderland. No one else has ever been able to see
it. No one else has ever been able to go there. Not even I
can ever return to it physically; it lies thirty-eight years in
the past, in the eye-level perspective of a child, its ster-
eoscopic accuracy based on the separation between the eyes
of a child. In only one place does it actually exist. In my
mind, Elizabeth—in *my* life. But I will die, and where will
it be, then?"

Elizabeth looked up at him. "In my mind, a little? Along
with the rest of you?"

Hawks looked at her. He reached out, and bending forward as tenderly as a child receiving a snowflake to hold,
gently enclosed her in his arms. "Elizabeth, Elizabeth," he
said. "I never realized what you were letting me do."

"I love you."

They walked together down the beach. "When I was a
little girl," she said, "my mother registered me with Central
Casting and tried to get me parts in the movies. I remember,
one day there was a call for someone to play the part of a
Mexican sheepherder's daughter, and my mother very carefully dressed me in a little peasant blouse and a flowered
skirt, and bought a rosary for me to hold. She braided my
hair, and darkened my eyebrows, and took me down to the
studio. When we got back to the house that afternoon, my
aunt said to my mother, 'Didn't get it, huh,' and my mother,

who was in a tearful fury, said, 'It was the lousiest thing I've ever seen! It was terrible! She almost had it, but she got beaten out by some little Spic brat!'"

Hawks tightened the arm he held around her shoulders. He looked out to sea, and at the sky. "This is a beautiful place!" he said. "You know, this is a beautiful place."

NINE

Barker was leaning against a cabinet when Hawks came into the laboratory in the morning and walked up to him.

"How do you feel?" Hawks asked, looking sharply at him. "All right?"

Barker smiled faintly. "What do you want to do? Touch gloves before we start the last round?"

"I asked you a question."

"I'm fine. Full of piss and vinegar. O.K., Hawks? What do you want me to tell you? That I'm all choked up with pride? That I know this is an enormous step forward in science, in which I am honored to find myself participating on this auspicious day? I already got the Purple Heart, Doc—just gimme a coupla aspirin."

Hawks said earnestly, "Barker, are you quite sure you'll be able to come out through the other side of the formation?"

"How can I be sure? Maybe part of its logic is that you can't win. Maybe it'll kill me out of simple spite. I can't tell about that. All I can promise you is that I'm a move away from the end of the only safe pathway. If my next move doesn't get me outside, then there isn't any way out. It *is* a tomato can, and I've hit bottom. But if it's something else, then, yes, today is the day; the time is now."

Hawks nodded. "That's all I can ask of you. Thank you." He looked around. "Is Gersten at the transmitter?"

Barker nodded. "He told me we'd be ready to shoot in about half an hour."

Hawks nodded. "All right. Fine. You might as well get into your undersuits. But there'll be some delay. We're going to have to take a preliminary scan on myself, first. I'm going along with you."

Barker ground out his cigarette under his heel. He looked up. "I suppose I should say something about it. Some kind of sarcastic remark about wading intrepidly into the hostile shore after the troops have already taken the island. But I'll be damned if I thought you'd do it at all."

Hawks said nothing, and walked away across the laboratory floor toward the transmitter.

"You knew we had extra suits," he said to Gersten, as he lay down in the opened armor. The Navy men worked around him, adjusting the set-screws on the pressure plates. The ensign stood watching closely, an uncertain frown on his face.

"Yes, but that was only in case we lost one in a bad scan," Gersten argued, his eyes stubborn.

"We've always had a stock of equipment, in all sizes."

"Hawks, being able to do something, and doing it, are two different things. I—"

"Look, you know the situation. You know what we're doing here as well as I do. Once we have a safe pathway, the probing and the study really begin. We're going to have to disassemble that thing like a bomb; I'm in charge of the project. Up to now, if I were lost to the project, it would have been too much of an expenditure. But now the risk is acceptable. I want to see what that thing's like. I want to be able to give intelligent directions. Is that so hard to understand?"

"Hawks, any number of things could still go wrong up there today."

"Suppose they don't. Suppose Barker makes it. Then what? Then he stands there, and I'm down here. Do you think I wasn't planning to do this, from the very beginning?"

"Even before you knew Barker?"

"I wish I'd never known Barker. Stand aside and let them close the armor." He fitted his left hand carefully into its gauntlet inside its tool cluster.

He was wheeled into the chamber. The magnets took hold, and the table was pulled out. The door closed and was dogged shut. He floated in mid-air, his legs and arms outspread, surrounded by the hundred thousand glittering eyes of the scanner faces. He lay looking up through the circle of glass in his helmet, his face expressionless. "Any time, Ted," he said sleepily into his microphone, and the chamber lights winked out.

The lights came on in the receiver. He opened his eyes, blinking gently. The receiver door was opened, and the table was slipped under him. The lateral magnets slacked off as their rheostats were turned down, and he drifted into contact with the plastic surface. "I feel normal," he said. "Did you get a good file tape?"

"As far as we know," Gersten said into his microphone. "The computers didn't spot any breaks in the transmission."

"Well, that's as well as we can do," Hawks said. "All right—put me back in the transmitter, and hold me there. Get Barker into his suit, jack down the legs on the table, and slide him in under me. Today," he said, "marks another precedent in the annals of exploration. Today, we're going to send a sandwich to the Moon."

Fidanzato, wheeling the table across the laboratory floor, laughed nervously. Gersten jerked his head to the side and looked at him.

2

Hawks and Barker climbed slowly to their feet in the Moon receiver. The Navy specialists waiting outside now opened the door, and stood aside to let them clamber out. The Moon station was bare and gray, with triangular plastic geodesic girders webbing the semiflexible sheet roof of the dome. Lights were hung from it at intervals, like stalactites, and the floor was a sieve of pressed matting over a ground sheet. Hawks looked around him curiously, the helmet of his armor swiveling with a faint grating sound that was instantly taken up by the fabric of the dome and amplified, so that every move each man made was followed by its larger echo. The interior of the building was never still. It creaked and groaned constantly, shivering the lights on their hangers; the group of men—the Navy crew in their under-suits and Hawks and Barker in their armor—were bathed in shifting reflections as though they were at the bottom of a sea beset by a powerful storm above them. At the airlock, the Navy men got back into their own rubberized canvas suits, and then, one by one, they all stepped out onto the open surface of the Moon.

Starlight shone down upon them with cold, drab intensity, stronger than anything falling from a moonless sky upon the Earth at night, but punched through with sharp rents of shadows at every hump and jag of the terrain. From ground level, it was possible to make out the vague shapes of the working naval installation, each dome and burrow with its latticework of overhead camouflage, lying like the wreck of a zeppelin to Hawks' right, looking vaguely gray-green in color, with no lights showing.

Hawks took a deep breath. "All right, thank you," he said to the Navy men, his voice distant, mechanical, and businesslike over the radio telephone circuit. "Are the ob-server teams ready?"

A Navy man, with lieutenant's bars painted on his hel-met, nodded and gestured toward the left. Hawks turned his head slowly, his expression reluctant, and looked to where the humps of the observation bunker clustered as though huddled in the lee of a cliff, at the foot of the looming black and silver formation.

"The walkway's over here," Barker said, touching Hawks' forearm with the tool cluster at the end of his right sleeve.

"Let's go—we'll run out of air if we wait for you to dip your toe in the water."

"All right." Hawks moved to follow Barker under the camouflage roofing which followed, like a pergola on which no vines would climb, above the track which had been smoothed for a footpath between the receiver dome and the formation.

The Navy lieutenant made a hand signal of dismissal and began to walk away, followed by his working party, taking the other path which led back to their station and their workaday concerns.

"All set?" Barker asked when they reached the formation. "Flash your light toward the observers, there, so they'll know we're starting."

Hawks raised one of his hands and winked its work light. An acknowledging point of light appeared upon the featureless black face of the bunker.

"That's all there is to it, Hawks. I don't know what you're waiting for. Just do what I do, and follow me. Let's hope this gizmo doesn't mind my not being alone."

"That's an acceptable risk," Hawks said.

"If you say so, Doctor." Barker put his arms out and placed the inner faces of his sleeves against the rippling, glossy wall at which the walkway came to a dead end. He shuffled sideways and there was a sharp *spang!* inside Hawk's armor, cracking up through his bootsoles, as the wall accepted Barker and sucked him through.

Hawks looked down at the loose gravel of the walkway, covered with bootprints as though an army had marched past. He came up to the wall and raised his arms, perspiration running down his cheeks faster than the suit's dehumidifiers could dry it.

3

Barker was scrambling up a tilting plane of glittering blue-black, toward where two faces of coarse dull brown thudded together repeatedly. Curtains of green and white swirled around Hawks. He broke into a run, as shafts of crystal transparency opened through the folds of green and white, with flickering red light dimly visible at their far ends and blue, green, yellow heaving upward underfoot.

Hawks ran with his arms pressed to his sides. He came to where he had seen Barker dive forward, rolling over as he skittered to the side along the running stream of yielding, leaflike pale fringes. As he dove, he passed over a twisted body in a type of armor that had been discarded.

Barker's white armor suddenly bloomed with frost which scaled off as he ran and lay in Hawks' way like molds of the equipment, in a heap of previous sleeves, legs, and torsos, to which Hawks' armor added its own as he passed.

Hawks followed Barker down the spiraling funnel whose walls smeared them with light gray powder which fell from their armor slowly, in long, delicate strands, as they swung themselves out to pass Rogan's body, which lay half out of sight in a heap of glazed semicircles like a shipment of broken saucers that had been discarded.

Barker held up his hand, and they stopped at the edge of the field of crosshatched planes, standing together, looking into each other's faces below the overhang of the polished tongue of blue-black metal which jutted out above them, rusted a coarse dull brown where an earlier Barker had once crawled out on it and now lay sprawled with one white sleeve dangling, a scrap of green surfacing clutched in the convulsively jammed pincers of his tool cluster. Barker looked up at it, back at Hawks, and winked. Then he took hold of one of the crystalline, transparent projections jutting out from the flickering red wall and swung himself out toward the next one, passing out of sight around the bend where blue, green, yellow light could be seen streaming.

Hawks' armored feet pattered at the empty air as he followed around the corner. He went hand-over-hand, carefully keeping his body strained upward to keep his shoulders above the level of his hands as he moved sideward along the high, scalloped coaming of pale yellow, each half-curved leaf yielding waxily to his weight and twisting down almost to where his pincers lost their grip on the surface, which their needle points could not penetrate. He had to cross his arms and shift his weight from each scallop to the next before it had time to drop him, and as he moved along he had to twist his body to avoid the spring-back of each half-saucer from which his grip had been discarded. Down below lay a tangle of broken armor; twisted sleeves and legs and torsos.

Hawks came, eventually, to where Barker lay on his

back, resting. He began to sit down beside him, lowering himself awkwardly. Suddenly he threw a glance at his wrist, where the miniaturized gyrocompass pointed at lunar north. He twisted his body, trying to regain his balance, and finally stood panting, on one foot like a water bird, while Barker steadied him. Overhead, orange traceries flickered through a glassy red mass shaped like a giant rat's head, and then reluctantly subsided.

They walked along an enormous, featureless plain of panchromatic grays and blacks, following a particular line of footprints among a fan of individual tracks. All of them ended in a huddle of white armor except for this one, on which Barker would stop, now and then, just short of his own corpse each time, and step to one side, or simply wait a bit, or shuffle by to the side. Each time he did so, the plain would suddenly flicker back into color from Hawks' point of view. Each time he followed Barker's lead, the color would die, and his suit would thrum with a banging, wooden sound.

At the end of the plain was a wall. Hawks looked at his wrist watch. Their elapsed time inside the formation was four minutes, fifty-one seconds. The wall shimmered and bubbled from their feet up into the black sky with its fans of violet light. Flowers of frost rose up out of the plain where their shadows fell, standing highest where they were farthest from the edges and so least in contact with the light. The frost formed humped, crude white copies of their armor, and, as Hawks and Barker moved against the wall, it lay for one moment open and exposed, then burst silently from steam pressure, each outflying fragment of discard trailing a long, delicate strand of steam as it ate itself up and the entire explosion reluctantly subsided.

Barker struck the wall with a sharp rock-hammer, and a glittering blue-black cube of its substance sprang away from it, exposing a coarse brown flat surface. Barker tapped lightly, and it changed color to a glittering white alive with twisting green threads. The facing of the wall turned crystalline and transparent, and disappeared. They stood on the lip of a lake of smoking red fire. On its shore, half-buried, the white paint sooted yellow, charred and molten so that it had run like a cheap crockery glaze, lay Barker's armor. Hawks looked at his wrist watch. Their elapsed time inside the formation was six minutes, thirty-eight seconds. He turned and looked back. On the open, panchromatic plain lay a featureless cube of metal, glittering blue-black. Barker turned back, picked it up, and threw it down on the ground. A coarse brown wall rose up into the air between them and the plain, and behind them the fire snuffed out. Where Barker's burnt armor had been was heap of crystals at the edge of a square, perhaps a hundred meters to one side, of lapis lazuli.

Barker stepped out on it. A section of the square tilted, and the crystals at its edge slid out across it in a glittering fan. Barker walked down carefully among them, until he was at the other edge of the section, steadying it with his weight. Hawks climbed up onto the slope and walked down to join him. Barker pointed. Through the crack between the section and the remainder of the square, they could see men from the observation team, peering blindly in at them. Hawks looked at his wrist watch. Their elapsed time inside the formation was six minutes, thirty-nine seconds. Lying heaped and barely visible between them and the observation team was Barker. The crystals on their section were sliding off into the crack and falling in long, delicate strands of snow upon the dimly-seen armor.

Barker clambered up onto the lazuli square. Hawks followed him, and the section righted itself behind them. They walked out for several meters, and Barker stopped. His face was strained. His eyes were shining with exhilaration. He glanced sideward at Hawks, and his expression grew wary.

Hawks looked pointedly down at his wrist watch. Barker licked his lips, then turned and began to run in a broadening spiral, his boots scuffing up heaps of crystals, at each of which he ducked his head as waves of red, green, yellow light dyed his armor. Hawks followed him, the lazuli cracking out in great radiations of icy fractures that crisscrossed into a network under his feet as he ran around and around.

The lazuli turned steel-blue and transparent, and then was gone, leaving only the net of fractures, on which Barker and Hawks ran, while below them lay the snowed armor and the observing team standing oblivious a few inches from it, and the stars and jagged horizon of the Moon behind them, a broken face against which the arc of the sky was fitted.

Their elapsed time inside the formation was nine minutes, nineteen seconds. Barker stopped again, his feet and pincers hooked in the network, hanging motionless, looking back over his shoulder as Hawks came up. Barker's eyes were desperate. He was breathing in gasps, his mouth working. Hawks clambered to a stop beside him.

The net of fractures began to break into dagger-pointed shards, falling away, leaving great rotten gaps through which swirled clouds of steel-gray, smoky particles which formed knife-sharp layers and hung in the great open space above the footing to which Hawks and Barker clung, and whose fringes whirled up and across to interlock the layers into a grid of stony, cleavage-planed crosshatchings which advanced toward them.

Barker suddenly closed his eyes, shook his head violently in its casque, blinked, and, with a tearful grimace, began to climb up the net, holding his left arm pressed against his side, clutching above him for a new handhold with his right as soon as his weight was off each toehold which his left foot discarded.

When Hawks and Barker emerged at the rim of the net, beside the drifted armor which lay under its crust of broken dagger-points, their elapsed time inside the formation was nine minutes, forty-two seconds. Barker faced the observing team through the wall, and stepped out onto the open Moon. Hawks followed him. They stood looking at each other through their faceplates, the formation directly behind them.

Barker looked at it. "It doesn't look as if it knows what we've done," he said over the radiotelephone circuit.

Hawks cast a glance behind him. "Did you expect it to?" he shrugged. He turned to the men of the observer team who were standing, waiting, in their moonsuits, their faces patient behind the transparent plastic bubbles of their helmets.

"Did you gentlemen see anything new happen while we were in there?"

The oldest man on the team, a gray-faced, drawn individual whose steel-rimmed spectacles were fastened to an elastic headband, shook his head. "No." His voice came distorted through his throat microphone. "The formation shows no outward sign of discriminating between one individual and another, or of reacting in any special way to the presence of more than one individual. That is, I suppose, assuming all its internal strictures are adhered to."

Hawks nodded. "That was my impression, too." He turned toward Barker. "That very likely means we can now begin sending technical teams into it. I think you've done your job, Al. I really think you have. Well, let's come along with these gentlemen, here, for a while. We might as well give them our verbal reports, just in case Hawks and Barker L had lost contact with us before we came out." He began to walk along the footpath toward the observation bunker, and the others fell in behind him.

4

Gersten knelt down and bent over the opened faceplate. "Are you all right, Hawks?" he asked.

Hawks L looked muzzily up at him. There was a trickle of blood running out of the corner of his mouth. He licked at it, running his tongue over the bitten places in his lower lip. "Must have been more frightened than I thought, after M drifted away from me and I realized I was in the suit." He rolled his head from side to side, lying on the laboratory floor. "Barker all right?"

"They're getting him out of the receiver now. He seems to be in good shape. Did you make it, all right?"

Hawks L nodded. "Oh, yes, that went well. The last I felt of M, he was giving the observation team a verbal report." He blinked to clear his eyes. "That's quite a place, up there. Listen——Gersten——" He looked up, his face wrinkled into an expression of distaste as he looked at the man. When he was a boy, and suffering from a series of heavy colds, his father had tried to cure them by giving him scalding baths and then wrapping him in wet sheets, drawing each layer tight as he wound it around Eddie Hawks' body and over his arms, leaving the boy, in this manner, pinned in overnight. "I——I hate to ask this," he said, not realizing that his face was turned directly up at Gersten, "but do you suppose the crew could get me out of my suit before they do Barker?"

Gersten, who had at first been watching Hawks with interest and concern, had by now become completely frigid and offended. "Of course," he said and stalked away, leaving Hawks L alone on the floor, like a child in the night. He lay that way for several moments before one of the technicians who stood in a ring around him realized he might want company and knelt down beside him, in range of the restricted field of vision through the faceplate opening.

5

Hawks M watched the chief observer close his notebook. "I think that does it, then," he said to the man. Barker, who was sitting beside him at the steel table, nodded hesitantly.

"I didn't see any lake of fire," he said to Hawks.

Hawks shrugged. "I didn't see any jagged green glass archway in its place." He stood up and said to the observer team, "If you gentlemen would please refasten our face-plates for us, we'll be on our way."

The observers nodded and stepped forward. When they were done they turned and left the room through the airtight hatch to the bunker's interior, so that Hawks and Barker were left alone to use the exterior airlock. Hawks motioned impatiently as the demand valve in his helmet began to draw air from his tanks again, its sigh filling his helmet. "Come along, Al," he said. "We don't have much time."

Barker said bitterly as they circled through the lock, "It sure is good to have people make a fuss over you and slap you on the back when you've done something."

Hawks shook his head. "These people, here, have no concern with us as individuals. Perhaps they should have had, today, but the habit would have been a bad one to break. Don't forget, Al—to them, you've never been anything but a shadow in the night. Only the latest of many shadows. And other men will come up here to die. There'll be times when the technicians slip up. There may be some reason why even you or perhaps even I, will have to return here. These men in this bunker will watch, will record what they see, will do their best to help pry information out of this thing—" He gestured toward the obsidian hulk, toppling perpetually, perpetually reerecting itself, shifting in place, looming over the bunker, now reflecting the light of the stars, now dead black and lusterless. "This enormous puzzle. But you and I, Al, are only a species of tool, to them. It has to be that way. They have to live here until one day when the last technician takes the last piece of this thing apart. And then, when that happens, these people in this bunker will have to face something they've been trying not to think about all this time."

Hawks and Barker moved along the footpath.

"You know, Hawks," Barker said uncomfortably, "I almost didn't want to come out."

"I know."

Barker gestured indecisively. "It was the damnedest thing. I almost led us into the trap that caught me last time. And then I almost just stayed put and waited for it to get us. Hawks, I just—I don't know. I didn't want to come out. I had the feeling I was going to lose something. What, I don't know. But I stood there, and suddenly I knew there was something precious that was going to be lost if I came back out onto the Moon."

Hawks, walking steadily beside Barker, turned his head to look at him for the first time since they had left the bunker. "And did you lose it?"

"I—I don't know. I'll have to think about it for a long time, I think. I feel different. I can tell that much." Barker's voice grew animated. "I do."

"Is this the first time you've ever done something no other man has done before? Done it successfully, I mean?"

"I—well, no, I've broken records of one kind or another, and—"

"Other men had broken records at the same things, Al."

Barker stopped, and looked at Hawks. "I think that's it," he frowned. "I think you're right. I've done something no other man has ever done before. And I didn't get killed for it."

"No precedent and no tradition, Al, but you did it anyway." Hawks, too, had stopped. "Perhaps you've become a man in your own right?" His voice was quiet, and sad.

"I may have, Hawks!" Barker said excitedly. "Look—you can't—That is, it's not possible to take in something like this all at once—but—" He stopped again, his face looking out eagerly through his faceplate.

They had come almost to the point where the footpath from the bunker joined the system of paths that webbed the terrain between the formation, the receiver, the Navy installation, and the motor pool where the exploration half-tracks stood. Hawks waited, motionless, patiently watching Barker, his helmet bowed as he peered.

"You were *right*, Hawks!" Barker said in a rush of words. "Passing initiations doesn't mean a thing, if you go right back to what you were doing before; if you don't *know* you've changed! A man—a man makes himself. He—Oh, God *damn* it, Hawks, I tried to be what *they* wanted, and I tried to be what I thought I *should* be, but what *am* I? That's what I've got to find out—that's what I've got to make something of! I've got to go back to Earth and straighten out all those *years*! I—Hawks, I'm probably going to be damned grateful to you."

"Will you?" Hawks began walking again. "Come with me, Al."

Barker trotted after him. "Where are you going?"

Hawks continued to walk until he was on the track that led toward the motor pool, and that continued past it for a short distance before the camouflaging stopped and the naked terrain lay nearly impassable to an armored man on foot. He waved shortly with one arm. "Out that way."

"Aren't you taking a chance? How much air is there in these suits?"

"Not much. A few minutes' more."

"Well, let's get back to the receiver, then."

Hawks shook his head. "No. That's not for us, Al."

"What do you mean? The return transmitter's working, isn't it?"

"It's working. But we can't use it."

"Hawks—"

"If you want to go to the transmitter and have the Navy crew go through the same procedure that sends samples and reports back to Earth, you can. But first I want you to understand what you'd be doing."

Barker looked at him in bewilderment through the thick glass. Hawks reached out and awkwardly touched his right sleeve to the man's armored shoulder. "Long ago, I told you I'd kill you in many ways, Al. When each Barker L came back to consciousness on Earth after each Barker M died, I was letting you trick yourself. You thought then you'd already felt the surest death of all. You hadn't. I have to do it once more.

"There was always a continuity. Barker M and L seemed to be the same man, with the same mind. When M died,

L simply went on. The thread was unbroken, and you could continue to believe that nothing, really, had happened. I could tell you, and you could believe, that in fact there was only a succession of Barkers whose memories dovetailed perfectly. But that's too abstract a thing for a human being to really grasp. At this moment, I think of myself as the Hawks who was born, years ago, in the bedroom of a farm home. Even though I know there's another Hawks, down in the laboratory on Earth, who's been living his own life for some moments, now; even though I know I was born from the ashes of this world twenty minutes ago, in the receiver. All that means nothing to the me who has lived in my mind all these years. I can look back. I can remember.

"That's the way it was with you, too. I told you. Long ago, I told you that the transmitter sends nothing but a signal. That it destroys the man it scans to derive that signal. But I knew as I told you that all the talk in the world wouldn't make you *feel* it that way, as long as you could wake up each morning in your own skin. So I suppose I was wasting all that talk. I often feel that I do. But what could I say to myself, now, if I hadn't tried to tell you?"

Barker said, "Get to the point!"

Hawks burst out in exasperation. "I'm *trying* to! I wish people would get it through their heads, once and for all, that the short answer is only good for familiar questions! What do you think we're dealing with, here—something Leonardo da Vinci could have handled? If he could have, he would have, and we would have had the Twentieth Century in Fifteen Hundred! If you want the answer at all, then you'd better let me put it in context."

"All right, Hawks."

"I'm sorry," Hawks said, the flare dying down. "I'm sorry. A man has things bottled up inside him, and they come out, in the end. Look, Barker—it's simply that we don't have the facilities here for accurately returning individuals to Earth. We don't have the computing equipment, we don't have the electronic hardware, we don't have any of the elaborate safeguards. We will have. Soon we'll have hollowed out a chamber large enough to hold them underground, where they'll be safe from accidents as well as observation. Then we'll either have to pressurize the entire chamber or learn to design electronic components that'll work in a vacuum. And if you think that's not a problem, you're wrong. But we'll solve it. When we have time.

"There's been no *time*, Al. These people here—the Navy men, the observers—think of them. They're the best people for their jobs. Competent people. Competent people have families, careers, interests, properties of one kind or another; it's a fallacy to think that a man who makes a good astronomer, or a good cartographer, isn't good at many other areas of life. Some of them aren't. Most of them are. And all of them here know that when they came up here, counterparts of theirs stayed behind on Earth. They had to. We couldn't drain men like those away from their jobs. We couldn't risk having them die—no one knew what might happen up here. Terrible things still might. They all volunteered to come up here. They all understood. Back on Earth, their counterparts are going

on as though nothing had happened. There was one afternoon in which they spent a few hours in the laboratory,
of course, but that's already a minor part of their past,
for them.

"All of us up here are shadows, Al. But they're a
particular kind. Even if we had the equipment, they couldn't
go back. When we do get it, they still won't be able to.
We won't stop them if they want to try, but think, Al,
about that man who leads the observation team. Back on
Earth, his counterpart is pursuing a complicated scientific
career. He's accomplished a lot since the day he was
duplicated. He has a career, a reputation, a whole body
of experience which this individual, up here, no longer
shares. And the man here has changed, too—he knows
things the other doesn't. *He* has a whole body of divergent
experience. If he goes back, which of them does what?
Who gets the career, who gets the family, who gets the
bank account? They can try to work it out, if they want
to. But it'll be years, up here, before this assignment is
over. There'll have been divorces, births, deaths, mar-
riages, promotions, degrees, jail sentences, diseases—No,
most of them won't go back. But when this ends, where
will they go? We'd better have something for them to do.
Away from Earth—away from the world that has no room
for them. We've created a whole corps of men with the
strongest possible ties to Earth, and no future except in
space. But where will they go? Mars? Venus? We don't
have rockets that will drop receivers for them there. We'd
better have—but suppose some of them have become so
valuable we don't dare not duplicate them again? Then
what?

"You called them zombies, once. You were right. They're the living dead, and they know it. And they were made, by me, because there wasn't *time*. No time to do this systematically, to think this out in all its aspects, to comb the world for men we could use without subjecting them to this disruption. And for you and me, now, Al, there's the simple fact that we have a few minutes' air left in our suits and we can't go back, at all."

"For Pete's sake, Hawks, we can walk into any one of these bubbles, here, and get all the air we want!"

Hawks asked slowly, "And settle down and stay here, you mean, and go back in a year or two? You can if you want to, I suppose. What will you do, in that time? Learn to do something useful, here, wondering what you've been doing meanwhile, on Earth?"

Barker said nothing for a moment. Then he said, "You mean, I'm stuck here." His voice was quiet. "I'm a zombie. Well, is that bad? Is that worse than dying?"

"I don't know," Hawks answered. "You could talk to these people up here about it. They don't know, either. They've been thinking about it for some time. Why do you think they shunned you, Barker? Because there was nothing about you that frightened them more than they could safely bear? We had our wave of suicides after they first came up. The ones who're left are comparatively stable on the subject. But they stay that way because they've learned to think about it only in certain ways. But go ahead. You'll be able to work something out."

"But, Hawks, I want to go back to *Earth*!"

"To the world in your memories, that you want to remake?"

"Why *can't* I use the return transmitter?"

Hawks said, "I told you. We only have a transmitter up here. We don't have a laboratory full of control equipment. The transmitter here pulses signals describing the typewritten reports and rock samples the Navy crew put in the receiver. It isn't used much for anything, but when it is, that's what it carries. From here—without dead-accurate astronomical data, without our power supply—the signals spread, they miss our antenna down there, they turn to hash in the ionization layers—you just can't do, from the surface of an uninhabited, unexplored, airless satellite, what we can do from there. You can't just send up, from a world with Terrestrial gravity, with an atmosphere, with air pressure, with a different temperature range, equipment that will function here. It has to be designed for here and better yet, built here. Out of what? In what factory? It doesn't matter, with marks on paper and lumps of rock, that we've got the bare minimum of equipment we *had* to have time to adapt. By trial and error, and constant repetition, we push the signals through, and decipher them on Earth. If they're hashed up, we send a message to that effect, and a Navy yeoman types up a new report from his file carbon, and a geologist chips off another rock of the same kind. But a man, Barker—I told you. A man is a phoenix. We simply don't have the facilities here to take scan readings on him, feed them through differential amplifiers, cross-check, and make a file tape to recheck against.

"You can try it, Al. You can get into the return transmitter, and the Navy men will pull the switches. They've done it before, for other men who had to try it. As always, the scanner will destroy you painlessly and instantaneously. But what arrives on Earth, Al—what arrives on Earth is also not the man you've become since you were last put in the laboratory transmitter. I guarantee you that, Al."

Hawks raised his arms and dropped them. "Now do you see what I've done to you? Do you see what I've done to poor Sam Latourette, who'll wake up one day in a world full of strangers, never knowing what I did to him after I put him into the amplifiers, only knowing that now he'll be cured but his old, good friend, Ed Hawks, has died and gone to dust? I haven't played fair with any of you. I've never once shown any of you mercy, except now and then by coincidence."

He turned and began to walk away.

"Wait! Hawks—You don't have to—"

Hawks said, without stopping or turning his head, walking steadily, "What don't I have to? There's an Ed Hawks in the universe who remembers all his life, even the time he spent in the Moon formation, up to this very moment as he stands down in the laboratory. What's being lost? There's no expenditure. I wish you well, Al—you'd better hurry and get to that airlock. Either the one at the return transmitter or the one at the naval station. It's about the same distance, either way."

"Hawks!"

"I have to get out of these people's way," Hawks said abstractedly. "It's not part of their job to deal with corpses on their grounds. I want to get out there among the rocks."

He walked to the end of the path, the camouflaging's shadows mottling his armor, cutting up the outlines of his body until he seemed to become only another jagged, broken portion of the place through which he walked.

Then he emerged into the starlight, and his armour flashed with the clear, cold reflection.

"Hawks," Barker said in a muffled voice, "I'm at the airlock."

"Good luck, Barker."

Hawks clambered over the rocks until he began to pant. Then he stood, wedged in place. He turned his face up, and stars glinted on the glass. He took one shallow breath after another, more and more quickly. His eyes watered. Then he blinked sharply, viciously, repeatedly. "No," he said. "No, I'm not going to fall for that." He blinked again and again. "I'm not afraid of you," he said. "Someday I, or another man, will hold you in his hand."

6

Hawks L pulled off the orange undershirt over his head, and stood beside the dressing table, wearing nothing but the bottom of the suit, brushing at the talcum on his face and in his hair. His ribs stood out sharply under his skin.

"You ought to get out in the sun, Hawks," Barker said, sitting on the edge of the table, watching him.

"Yes," Hawks said abstractedly, thinking he had no way of knowing whether there really had been a plaid blanket on his bed in the farmhouse, or whether it had been a quilted comforter. "Well, I may. I should be able to find a little more time, now that things are going to be somewhat more routine. I may go swimming with a girl I know, or something. I don't know."

There was a note in his left hand, crumpled, and limp with perspiration, where he had been carrying it since before he was put into his armor the first time. He picked at it carefully, trying to open the folds without tearing them.

Barker asked, "Do you remember anything much about what happened to us on the Moon after we got through the formation?"

Hawks shook his head. "No, I lost contact with Hawks M shortly. And please try to remember that we have never been on the Moon."

Barker laughed. "All right. But what's the difference between being there and only remembering being there?"

Hawks mumbled, working at the note, "I don't know. Perhaps the Navy will have a report for us on what Hawks M and Barker M did afterward. That might tell us something. I rather think it will."

Barker laughed again. "You're a peculiar duck, Hawks."

Hawks looked at him sidelong. "That sums me up, does it? Well, I'm *not* Hawks. I remember being Hawks, but I was made in the receiver some twenty-five minutes ago, and you and I have never met before."

"All *right*, Hawks," Barker chuckled. "Relax!"

Hawks was no longer paying any attention to him. He opened the note, finally, and read the blurred message with little difficulty, since it was in his own handwriting and, in any case, he knew what it said. It was:

"Remember me to her."

QUESTAR®
... MEANS THE BEST SCIENCE FICTION AND THE MOST ENTHRALLING FANTASY.

Like all readers, science fiction and fantasy readers are looking for a good story. Questar® has them—entertaining, enlightening stories that will take readers beyond the farthest reaches of the galaxy, and into the deepest heart of fantasy. Whether it's awesome tales of intergalactic adventure and alien contact, or wondrous and beguiling stories of magic and epic quests, Questar® will delight readers of all ages and tastes.

___**PASSAGE AT ARMS**   *(E20-006, $2.95, U.S.A.)*
    by Glen Cook   *(E20-007, $3.75, Canada)*

A continuation of the universe Glen Cook develops in *The Starfishers Trilogy*, this is a wholly new story of an ex-officer-turned-reporter taking the almost suicidal assignment of covering an interstellar war from a tiny, front-line attack ship.

___**PANDORA'S GENES**   *(E20-004, $2.95, U.S.A.)*
    by Kathryn Lance   *(E20-005, $3.75, Canada)*

A first novel by a fresh new talent, this book combines a love triangle with a race to save humanity. In a post-holocaustal world, where technology is of the most primitive sort, a handful of scientists race against time to find a solution to the medical problem that may mean humanity's ultimate extinction.

___**THE DUSHAU TRILOGY #1: DUSHAU** *(E20-015, $2.95, U.S.A.)*
    by Jacqueline Lichtenberg   *(E20-016, $3.75, Canada)*

The Dushau see the end of a galactic civilization coming—but that's not surprising for a race of near-immortals whose living memory spans several thousand years. The newly crowned emperor of the Allegiancy wants to pin his troubles on Prince Jindigar and the Dushau, but Krinata, a plucky young woman who works with the Dushau, determines to aid their cause when she discovers the charges are false.

WARNER BOOKS
P.O. Box 690
New York, N.Y. 10019

Please send me the books I have checked. I enclose a check or money order (not cash), plus 50¢ per order and 50¢ per copy to cover postage and handling.* (Allow 4 weeks for delivery.)

_____ Please send me your free mail order catalog. (If ordering only the catalog, include a large self-addressed, stamped envelope.)

Name _____

Address _____

City _____

State _____ Zip _____

*N.Y. State and California residents add applicable sales tax.   135

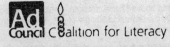